SADDLER

Ben Saddler, sometime soldier of the Confederate Army, has had many jobs: scout, gambler, barkeep, deputy sheriff, road agent, cowboy . . . Now he is a whiskey runner trying to scrape a living in the Indian Territories. His life takes an unexpected turn when he suddenly finds himself responsible for a young girl. Somehow, he must escort her to safety; evade capture by the law; outgun those who would kill him; and negotiate his way through an Indian uprising. Can he succeed?

Books by Harriet Cade
in the Linford Western Library:

THE HOMESTEADER'S DAUGHTER
THE MARSHAL'S DAUGHTER
TEACHER WITH A TIN STAR

HARRIET CADE

SADDLER'S
RUN

Complete and Unabridged

LINFORD
Leicester

First published in Great Britain in 2014 by
Robert Hale Limited
London

First Linford Edition
published 2016
by arrangement with
Robert Hale
an imprint of The Crowood Press
Wiltshire

A catalogue record for this book is available
from the British Library.

ISBN 978–1–4448–3075–0

Published by
F. A. Thorpe (Publishing)
Anstey, Leicestershire

Set by Words & Graphics Ltd.
Anstey, Leicestershire
Printed and bound in Great Britain by
T. J. International Ltd., Padstow, Cornwall

This book is printed on acid-free paper

1

Five years after the end of the great War between the States, there was still a considerable number of restless, fiddle-footed men drifting around the country who had fought in the war and now seemed unable to adjust to the peace. It was as though excitement, danger and the risk of death were potent drugs for which these men had acquired a taste during the four years of fighting and to which they were now hopelessly addicted. Some of them rejoined the army and took part in the Indian Wars, while others worked as lawmen and scouts. Then again, there were those who turned bad and took up as road agents or robbed banks. Mostly though, these rootless young men moved from place to place, working at whatever came along. Anything other than settling down and living humdrum and routine lives. One such, a fairly typical specimen of the breed, was Ben Saddler, sometime soldier of the Confederate Army and since then scout, gambler, barkeep, deputy sheriff, road agent, cowboy and now whiskey runner.

On a fine April morning in 1871, a light covered wagon was rattling along a dusty track leading into the Indian Territories. The driver was a lanky, fair-haired man in his late twenties who looked as though he had been around a bit. He was dressed in a pair of blue serge pants, faded and patched, and a buckskin shirt. There was a .36 cap-and-ball pistol tucked in his belt and a rifle lying on the buckboard at his feet.

At different times over the last twelvemonth or so, Ben Saddler had brought various illicit goods into the Indian Territories, ranging from moonshine liquor to rifles. In back of his wagon today were crates of whiskey, which he was hoping to exchange for horses.

The land hereabouts was scrubby and bleak, broken at intervals by patches of woodland, like the one ahead. Saddler reined in the horse and considered the stretch of forest through which he was about to pass. There had been ugly incidents in recent months of traders set upon and murdered for their goods and he did not aim to be another of those unfortunate cases. The wood looked a pretty fine spot for an ambush, if anybody had such a thing in mind. Reaching down for his rifle, Saddler brought it up, cocked it and set it upon his knees. Then he touched up the horses and set them towards the trees at a walk, rather than a trot.

Some hundred yards into the wood, Saddler knew that his cat's sense for danger had not played him false. A light wagon, smaller than his own and little more than a glorified buckboard, was blocking the road. It was not harnessed up to any horses and looked to him like a trap: a deliberate attempt to slow down any passing travellers, prior to robbing or killing them. Checking that his pistol was loose in his belt and bringing his rifle up ready for action, he pulled up ten yards or so from the wagon slewed across his way. Then he waited. Saddler's army comrades used to josh him that he must have had Indian blood in him, he was that good at just sitting in complete immobility until the time came to strike.

After sitting motionless for perhaps five minutes Saddler heard a soft rustling in the bushes to his right, as though someone was moving stealthily towards him. He brought the rifle up to his shoulder, took first pull upon the trigger and cried, 'Stand to, whoever you be, 'less you want a minie ball through your heart!'

The crackling in the undergrowth grew louder and just as he was about to fire, there came the greatest surprise of his whole, entire life when out from the bushes stepped a little girl.

She was a solemn-faced white girl,

wearing a long black dress. Her hair was neatly plaited and she could have been no more than ten or eleven years of age. The child looked up at him with wide eyes and said, 'Are you going to hurt me?'

'Nothin' o' the sort, honey, though you came pretty close to stopping a bullet from this here rifle o' mine. Step forward an' tell me how come you're wandering here.'

The girl made no move and Saddler realized that he still had his rifle pointing in her direction and ready to fire. He lowered it and then put it down entirely.

'Come on, now,' he said in a gentler voice, 'Don't be afeared. Nobody goin' to harm you.'

'They killed my mother and father,' said the child sadly, although without overmuch emotion, like she might have been mentioning the loss of a favourite doll. 'They stabbed them and then messed up their bodies. Why would they do that?'

His hackles began to rise again at the child's words. Saddler had just known that there was mischief afoot and hearing what this little girl said served only to confirm his suspicions. He jumped down in front of the girl and she winced fearfully, probably expecting him to attack her.

'You got no cause to fear me,' he said, 'I'll help you if I'm able. Where's your ma and pa?'

'Over yonder,' said the child, 'They dragged them off the road after they was killed and then did stuff to them. I don't rightly mind what.'

'Stay here, now. I'll see what's what.'

He went over to the other wagon and soon found what he was looking for. Just off the road were the bodies of a man and woman. Both had been stabbed to death and then mutilated. He had seen such things before, more than once, but it still made him grimace. There was a sound behind him and Saddler turned to find that the child had followed him and was staring dispassionately at the bodies of her parents.

'Come away,' he said. 'This ain't a fittin' sight for you.' He led her back to his own wagon, glancing in to the back of the cart straddling the track. There were wooden boxes inside, which had been carelessly smashed open and the contents strewn everywhere. There looked to be only books and he picked one up and leafed through it. It was a Bible.

When they got back to his own wagon he lifted the little girl up on to the seat and then climbed up beside her. 'What's with all them Bibles?' he asked.

'My mother and father were taking them into the territories. They were for the heathens who live there.'

'Missioners, hey? How come you didn't fall prey to the same fate as them?'

The girl's face grew animated as she told the story. 'My father heard some riders coming up behind us. He had a

7

fear that something was amiss and so he told me to jump down and hide in the bushes until he knew what the case was.'

'Well,' said Saddler. 'And what was the case?'

'It was a bunch of Indians. They did not stop to parley, just lit right in and killed them. I was hiding and watched the whole thing.'

'When was this? How long ago, I mean?'

'It was yesterday. I have been hiding ever since.'

'That's the hell of a thing for a little girl like you to go through,' he said.

'My father says that using 'hell' like that is what you call strong language,' said the girl, primly.

It was on the tip of Saddler's tongue to observe that not any more her father didn't, but just in time he recollected that he was speaking to a child who had just lost her folks.

Instead, he said, 'Truth to tell, I never thought 'hell' as being strong language. Leastways, I heard stronger.'

'My father says that bad language and such can lead to worse things later.'

'In my case,' said Saddler, 'the boot's on the other foot. I begun with the worse things until now I've ended up just cursing.' The ghost of a smile flickered on the girl's mouth and he felt pleased that he had taken her mind off the horror she had endured. 'Question is,' he mused, 'what's to be done with you now?'

'Oh, that's all right,' she said. 'Don't you see, the Lord has sent you to take care of me? Everything will be fine now.' Her face radiated complete and perfect confidence in Ben Saddler's ability and intention to tend to her needs.

'The Lord don't enter into the equation,' he said, ''Twas only chance fetched me up here, nothin' more.'

'That doesn't signify. The Lord uses all sort of folks. Just look at Jael the Kennite. In the Bible, you know.'

'That's nothing to the purpose,' said Saddler. 'Me and the Lord haven't been on good terms for some time. It ain't in reason that he'd ask now for my help. Still and all, I can't leave you here alone. There's a tradin' post a day's ride from here. I'll take you there an' leave you. They'll deal with this situation a sight better than I am able.'

After pushing the other wagon to one side, Saddler succeeded in manoeuvring his wagon past that of the dead missioners. He asked suddenly, 'What become o' the horse as drew that thing?'

'The Indians took it,' said the girl.

'I reckon I should introduce myself. My name is Saddler, Ben Saddler.'

'I am called Abigail, sir.'

'There's no occasion to call me sir. Ben's my name.'

They rode along for a space, Saddler brooding about the likelihood of an attack from the same crew who had killed the girl's parents, and the girl just sitting there with her hands folded in her lap. She did not fidget or chatter the way most children whom he had

encountered seemed to do. The pro-
longed silence did not appear to
discomfit her in the least degree, but it
began to irk Saddler, who remarked
after a space,

'For a child of your years who's lost
her ma and pa, strikes me as you're
mighty composed.'

'My father said that it was sinful to
grieve for good people who die,' said
Abigail. 'He said that if somebody has
been promoted to glory, then it is
heathenish to bewail their fate and cry
and suchlike.' She paused for a
moment, before adding, 'Anyways, we
are not much given to showing our
feelings in my family. I am grieved at
my loss, but there is nothing to be done
about it.'

This all seemed to Saddler positively
unnatural in one so young, but he knew
little enough of the ways of children
and so kept his own counsel.

For the next half-hour the two of
them sat silently as the wagon jolted
and bumped its way along the rough

track. There was no sign to indicate that they had entered the Indian Territories and so passed into another jurisdiction. The crates of liquor had, as they crossed the invisible border, undergone a sudden transformation; from being the legitimate possessions of a man partial to a drop of whiskey they had been transmuted into illegal contraband rendering the owner liable to imprisonment.

Saddler saw the party of horsemen heading straight towards them when they were still a couple of miles away. He said nothing, hoping that the girl had not noticed them. When the men were about a half-mile away they broke into a gallop, clearly intent upon intercepting the wagon. He picked up the rifle and cocked it.

'What are you doing?' said the child. 'Is that Indians coming this way?'

Saddler glanced at Abigail, whose face had gone chalky white. 'Don't fret,' he told her. 'Like as not they mean us no harm.'

As the Indians rode down on them the man in the lead raised his rifle and fired it one-handed into the air. The girl clutched at Saddler in fear and he clucked reassuringly. Then the whole group divided into two and swept past on either side of the wagon, giving blood-curdling war cries as they did so. They thundered off until after a spell there was silence again.

'Why didn't they attack us?' asked Abigail.

'Well, I know those boys.'

'They are friends of yours?'

'Hardly that,' said Saddler. 'I make no doubt that they'd cut my throat if they didn't need me. I sold 'em those rifles they was carrying.'

Abigail sat up and moved away from him. 'You are one of those who supply the Red Man with guns? My father had a deal to say about men such as you.'

He shrugged. 'A man has to make a livin' somehow.'

Abigail answered readily enough any questions that were asked of her, but essayed none of her own. This made conversation stilted and awkward and Saddler was not sorry when the trading post came into sight.

Scattered throughout the territories were various establishments whose owners somehow contrived to make a living from either the Indians or from the white men who had business in those parts. Some, such as the place where Saddler hoped to offload the child he had found, served the needs of both red and white men. The owner, Joe Abbot, bartered cheap pots, pans, utensils, tools and other ironmongery for hides and anything else the Indians might have to offer. He also ran a drinking den at the back for the convenience of passing white men.

Abbot's place was not like a regular saloon, but more like a Mexican cantina. It was little more than a dingy shack leaning against the stone wall of the dwelling-house where Abbot and his wife had their home. There was room for maybe a dozen men in there and most of those who frequented the place knew the others whom they saw there. A man might not visit for two or three months, but when he did drop in he was sure to see familiar faces. Nigh on all those who visited Abbot's place were living on the edge of the law as moonshiners, gun-runners and so on. They tended to trust only others of the same brand.

When Saddler walked through the door there was a moment's silence, a pause as those inside assured themselves that this was a known and trusted associate, rather than a stranger or, even worse, a lawman or soldier. As soon as they recognized Saddler there were boisterous shouts of welcome and invitations for him to come and join one or another group of the men seated round the tables. The noise died away utterly as they saw the neatly dressed little girl who followed him into the *cantina*.

Joe Abbot was serving food at the planks laid across two barrels that functioned as a bar in his place. He greeted Saddler affably enough, figuring that he would soon learn what the game was. It was the first time since he had opened this drinking hole that a child of such tender years had been seen there and, like everybody else, he was just itching to know how a man like Ben Saddler had come to be entrusted with the care of a minor.

The men at the tables resumed talking, but in a far more restrained and civil fashion. A minute earlier and both the content of their conversation and their mode of expressing themselves would have made a sailor blush. Now, the presence of a child — and a girl-child at that — caused them to moderate severely their language and conduct.

Abigail stood uncertainly in the doorway while Saddler talked to the owner of the bar. One of the men sitting at a nearby table coaxed her over and invited her to sit down. This fellow was a regular desperado, as villainous a type as you could wish to encounter, but in the presence of women and children he became as respectable as a parson.

'Come, little one,' he said. 'Sit here now and rest your feet.' Abigail smiled shyly and sat at his table.

Saddler was not having a deal of luck with his efforts to rid himself of his unwelcome charge.

'Truth is, Abbot, I need a favour . . . ' he began.

At the ominous word 'favour', Joe Abbot began shaking his head regretfully. 'If this talk of favours is tending towards the granting of credit or anything of that nature, then it will not answer. I am running this place at a loss already. Some of you boys seem to think that this is a charitable undertaking and I am like one of those wealthy philanthropists that you hear tell of. Sorry, Saddler, it can't be done.'

'Will you shut up a minute an' listen? This has no reference at all to money.'

This reassurance caused Abbot to fall

silent and see what would follow next.

'You see where I brought in a child with me?' said Saddler.

'I observed it,' replied the other warily.

'Now I found her a ways back, it don't matter how or where. She's an orphan an' in my line o' work, travelling hither and thither as you might say, I can't be expected to have a little girl tagging along with me. You must see that it's absurd?'

Abbot shrugged noncommittally. 'If you say so. It's no affair of mine who you take with you to your work.'

'That being so,' continued Saddler, 'I thought you might not mind allowin' the child to stay here with you for a spell. You could send her off with the next passing missioner.' He looked hopefully at Abbot, who was in turn staring at Saddler as though he had taken leave of his senses. Indeed, he intimated as much.

'You have been out in the sun too long, Saddler. Either that or you have lost your mind. It is not to be thought of. How the hell can I engage to look after a child here?'

'She might be useful to you. She could wait at tables an' such.'

'I am sorry not to oblige, Saddler. You are a good customer and have always dealt here pretty regular but I can't have a little girl here. No, it can't be done. There is an orphans' asylum at Greensborough. You could take her there.'

'Greensborough? I'd have to turn back the way I came an' then ride for the rest o' today and all tomorrow. Come on, Abbot, as an old friend, will you help me?'

'As an old friend, no I will not.'

There looked to be little chance of changing Abbot's mind on this topic and so Saddler went back to where Abigail was sitting and said roughly, 'Come on, we're leaving.'

The man who had invited her to sit by him said indignantly, 'The child is starving. Let her eat first.'

19

Saddler felt ashamed of himself, knowing that he should have thought of this for himself. The girl had wolfed down half a loaf of bread and so he went up and asked Abbot coldly if he could let them have some pork and beans. This dish was about all that was served here and there was always a steady supply.

While Abigail was eating, Saddler explained the setup to the others sitting at nearby tables, who, while agreeing that it was a crying shame, pointedly refused to become involved in the business. After the child had finished eating and drinking, Saddler led her outside and desired her to climb up on to the wagon. He looked up at her and said irritably, 'This is a damned nuisance.'

There was a discreet cough behind him and Saddler turned to find that one of the men had followed them out. It was a man he knew by sight but had not exchanged more than the usual civilities with. This fellow said,

'If you'll step over here to one side, I might be able to help with your problem.'

'How's that?' said Saddler, strolling with the man out of the child's earshot.

'What I propose is this,' said the man, who had to Saddlers' eye, a peculiarly ill-favoured look about him, 'I'll give you twenty-five dollars this minute and take charge of the girl. You then go on your way unencumbered.'

Saddler said nothing, but thought hard about this for a minute or so. Then he said,

'Something don't listen right 'bout this. Why'd you pay me to take the child?'

The other man smiled. 'There's no mystery. I'll take her south with me. Just over the border from El Paso there's places always on the scout for young girls. She's a little young yet, but they'd see she made herself useful 'til she's ready to . . . work.'

It has to be said that Ben Saddler was very far from being a saint, but when he grasped what was being suggested, he could scarcely believe what he had heard.

'What, you mean a cathouse?'

The other man smiled and nodded. Such an infamous suggestion deserved only one response and Saddler gave it swiftly, swinging his fist at the man's jaw and sending him sprawling in the dirt. As the man began to rise, it looked to Saddler as though he was about to go for the pistol at his hip. He pulled the pistol from his own belt, cocking the piece with his thumb as he did so, and drew down on the man.

'Touch that gun and you're a dead man,' said Saddler. 'You mangy cur, you'd buy an' sell a child like you would a horse or dog? I'm more than half minded to kill you this minute. Go back inside 'fore I change my mind.'

The odious wretch shuffled off and Saddler climbed on to the wagon and set off back the way he had come.

'What is to happen now?' asked Abigail in a quiet, scared voice.

'I'm takin' you to an orphans' asylum. We'll need to sleep out tonight an' with luck'll arrive tomorrow evening. It's a damned nuisance, but there's little else for it.'

They continued on until dusk, when Saddler halted the wagon and gave Abigail to understand that she could sleep in it with his blanket wrapped around her.

'If there is only one blanket, will you not be cold?' she asked.

'It's nothing,' said Saddler, 'I've slept without a blanket before.'

'I must say my prayers before sleeping. Will you say one with me?'

'I don't have time for such foolishness,' he replied. 'You say one on my behalf, if it comforts you any.'

Even after the girl was asleep, he could not settle. Speaking in general, Ben Saddler was not a one to let others dictate his actions. He felt obscurely that he had somehow been buffaloed into taking charge of this child and resented the imposition. But as to who or what it was that had pressed him against his will into undertaking this task, he was quite unable to offer even a tentative opinion.

2

Saddler awoke on the ground the next day, drenched in dew and in a thoroughly disagreeable frame of mind. He had hoped to dispose of his whiskey that day and to be leading a troop of ponies back across the border by nightfall. Instead, he had to double back on his tracks and visit Greensborough, where no doubt he would be compelled to answer a lot of damn fool questions before he could rid himself of the child. All in all, the circumstances were enough to make even the most equable and good-natured of individuals, into which category Saddler most definitely did not fall, a little tetchy.

Saddler's mood wasn't improved by the fact that he knew deep within his heart that he should not be embarking upon this course of action and that thought too was riling him up in no small measure.

He shook the girl's shoulder to wake her. She opened her eyes at once and for a moment her face seemed fresh and eager to face the day ahead. Then, recollecting perhaps the death of her parents, she appeared to Saddler to withdraw into herself again, putting on that same guarded, watchful and unemotional front that he had observed in her the previous day.

'We must be making tracks,' Saddler said. 'I aim to reach Greensborough this day and then you are going to the orphans' asylum.' He realized that he was speaking more harshly than was necessary and regretted his words almost as soon as they were out of his mouth. Abigail turned away from him and he feared for a moment that she was about to cry. She threw off the blanket and sat up.

'Is there anything to eat before we start?' she asked, her voice neutral and cool.

You're a rare customer and no mistake, thought Saddler to himself. You have seen your parents murdered in the most savage way imaginable and are about to be deposited in an orphanage, yet all you do is ask about breakfast.

'I've a couple o' rolls in my pack,' he told her. 'They're apt to be a little stale, but it's all we have.'

'Thank you,' said Abigail.

While they were eating Saddler asked the child, 'You got no other family as might take you in? If there's folks near Greensborough, then I guess I could take you there instead.' He did not really take to the scheme of leaving her in some institution, for all that he represented the case to her as a done deal.

'My father had no folks that I ever heard tell of,' said Abigail. 'My mother's people kind of disowned her when she got married to a missioner. Her father lives up in Kansas.' She named a small town in the south of that state.

'God almighty,' said Saddler, 'that's the better part of two hundred miles from here. I can't engage to take you that far. I've business to attend to. I dare say the orphans' asylum will write him.'

'I was not asking you to take me there,' Abigail said. 'You asked about my folks and I told you.'

Once again, Saddler was struck by how self-contained and aloof the child was. It was almost like talking to a grown-up person. I guess, he thought to himself, her parents raised her so.

After they ate the rolls, the two of them just sat there without speaking for a space, until Saddler announced abruptly, 'I growed up in an orphanage.'

'What . . . what was it like?' asked Abigail timidly.

'It was terrible,' he said. 'Just terrible.'

'Were they cruel to you?'

'That they were. Then again, there's the hunger. Never having a full belly.

Other things, I durst not tell you.'

The girl sat there, her face pinched and white; her eyes wide with dismay.

Saddler said, 'I would not deliver up a dog I liked to such a place. It won't answer. I can't take you to no damned orphans' asylum.'

Abigail said nothing and then asked, 'What will you do with me?'

'I reckon I'll have to take you to this grandpa o' yours. My conscience ain't exactly in tip-top condition, but I mind I'd never sleep easy again if I didn't make some attempt at aiding you.' Saddler smiled at the girl and said, 'Don't look sad, child. I ain't about to abandon you. I'm not such a dog as that.'

It was a fine day to be travelling across open country. The sun was shining and despite the fact that all his plans had been upset and he looked likely to waste the next few weeks on a fool's errand, Saddler found it hard to be out of sorts for long.

He said to the child at his side, 'Tell

me something about yourself. It ain't natural in a girl your age just to set there quietly in that way.'

'What would you like to know?'

'I don't know. How old are you?'

'I was twelve last month.'

'I took you for being younger,' said Saddler. 'You're small for your age.'

There was no reply and it looked as though there was going to be another long stretch of silence. It was not how Saddler liked to travel. He was a naturally sociable and gregarious sort, who liked to talk in order to idle away the time.

'Lord,' he said, 'making conversation with you is surely hard work. Don't you never chat about nothing in particular?'

Abigail did not answer and as the seconds passed, Saddler resigned himself to a journey spent as though he might as well have been alone. Then the girl said slowly,

'My father did not encourage me to speak just for the sake of it. He told me many times that if you have something worth saying, then you should say it and then when you have said it, you should stop speaking.'

'Begging your pa's pardon an' not wishin' to speak ill of him, but that's a lot o' nonsense. Why shouldn't we chat freely to each other? What other purpose in life is there, 'sides enjoyin' the company of others? That's hard to achieve if you all sit around without speaking.'

'I am not used to it. I do not mean to be sullen or aught like that. I am just not in the habit of talking a lot.'

'Well,' said Saddler, 'you are at any rate making a start now. Where'd you live, 'fore coming to the territories, I mean?'

'We moved about a lot. We did not spend long in one place. My father was about the Lord's business and that kept him busy in many different places. You never know where the Lord will send you.'

'What about school?'

'Oh, my father and mother taught me.'

'Did you have friends and suchlike though? Like you would in a school-room? I mean other children to play with.'

'I do not think I have had what you might call a friend. And my father said that playing was a waste of my time.'

And a right nice fellow your father sounds, thought Saddler to himself. Raising a little thing like this without friends and with no playing or ordinary chatter. No wonder she is so strange.

Abigail sensed what he was thinking, because she said suddenly, 'I would not have you think that my Pa was a cruel man or careless of my happiness. He and my mother loved me, but they were always thinking about the next world. They did not think much to this one.'

Now it was Saddler's turn to fall silent as he mulled over what she had said.

At length, he remarked bluntly, 'I can't say I take to that doctrine in anywise. Strikes me that a man who cannot get on in this world isn't likely

32

to do any better in the next. No offence meant to your pa, you understand.'

Little by little and with long periods of awkward silence, the two of them became tentatively acquainted as the morning drew on. By the time the sun was high in the sky, Saddler said,

'I guess we must think about procuring some food, or we're likely to go hungry 'til evening.'

The girl looked around the barren landscape and asked, 'Where shall we find food here? There are no stores or anything of that sort.'

Saddler laughed. 'Surely you are city-bred. I'll show you. I hope you ain't afeared o' loud noises?' He halted the wagon and they sat quietly for a minute or two. Saddler picked up his rifle and cocked it. While they had been travelling Abigail had seen jackrabbits hopping out of their way and now she realized that there were several near by, either grazing on the sparse and scanty grass or just sitting around and admiring the view. Without any warning the man at her side raised his rifle and fired. A plump jackrabbit leaped convulsively, hopped a little and then lay still.

'Scoot down and fetch that for me,' said Saddler.

'Won't it be all over blood?' asked Abigail.

'If you want to eat before dusk, you better fetch it here anyway.'

Abigail walked the twenty-five yards or so to the dead animal and picked it up, a look of disgust on her face. She managed to avoid getting any blood on her fingers. She climbed back on to the wagon and after another wait of ten minutes or so, Saddler repeated the trick. Then he sent the child over to a nearby clump of trees to gather kindling, while he gutted the animals; a messy job that he was not keen for Abigail to witness, seeing that she had seen her own parents served in similar fashion not forty-eight hours since.

Broiled jackrabbit makes a satisfying meal, especially if you have been out of doors all morning, having broken your fast on no more than a morsel of dry bread. They both felt sated and full by the time they set off again.

Now Saddler knew as well as anybody that the territories could be a hazardous place, most particularly when you were driving a wagon loaded up with a valuable commodity such as ardent spirits. He saw the two riders up ahead, apparently just sitting on their horses and admiring the view. There was little enough to see round that part of the country, other than the bleak, scrubby landscape, which consisted of nothing but dusty soil, low bushes and a few stunted trees. The hairs on the back of Saddler's neck rose the second he caught sight of them ahead; just loitering there by road.

'Why are you staring at those men up ahead?' asked Abigail.

'I mind they're up to no good,' replied Saddler shortly. 'You do just whatever I tell you now. Understand?'

'What would you have me do?'

'Nothing. Leastways, not yet a whiles. Just be ready to do as I say at once. If I say, get down, you get straight down an' crouch there on the buckboard. Or if I say, run, then you run. You got it?'

The girl wriggled closer to Saddler, as though sheltering from a cold wind. She said, 'Don't let them hurt me.'

There was something about the trusting tone in the child's voice that cut straight into Ben Saddler's heart. He looked down at Abigail and said,

'Anybody tries to hurt you, they soon goin' to learn their mistake. Don't fret now, it'll turn out all right.'

As they drew closer to the men on horseback Saddler realized that he knew one of them. Abraham Stock was not precisely a friend, but he and Saddler had done some business in the past. He wondered if Stock and his partner were up to the bushwhacking game and reached down to make sure that the rifle was right there at hand. When he was twenty yards from the two men

Saddler reined in and called to them,
    'What's to do, boys?'

Stock called back, 'Hey, Saddler. How goes it?'

'Just fine. What're you an' your partner about?'

Stock said, 'Come closer, man. We can't keep shouting so.'

Reaching down to the buckboard, Saddler picked up his rifle, cocking it unobtrusively as he did so. He said quietly to Abigail, 'You climb into the back of the wagon now, an' keep your head down.'

Saddler jumped down from the buckboard, with the rifle just held easy in his hand, like he might have picked it up as an afterthought. He walked slowly towards the two men on horseback, not taking his eyes from them for a moment. He halted a dozen feet away and asked,

    'Well, what're you two up to?'

'We ain't exactly up to anything,' said Abraham Stock, carefully. 'Truth is, we're in a bit of a fix and could do with a helping hand.'

Stock's companion said, 'What you got in the back of your wagon, friend?'

'I reckon that's my affair,' said Saddler curtly. 'You tend to your business and I'll look to mine.'

The man stared coldly at Saddler and said, 'That ain't what I would call a friendly approach.'

Stock intervened, apparently eager to smooth things over and avoid any unpleasantness.

'Fact is, Saddler,' he said, 'me and this fellow, whose name by the by is Joe Collins, have our tails in a crack. We're plumb out o' luck and money both and could surely do with your help.'

Without hearing another word, Saddler knew that this was going to end badly. Every so often those, like him, who made their living in this way would run out of money and goods and find themselves without any resources to fall back upon. Sometimes you could pull yourself back into credit by a little card play. Other times you were compelled to hire yourself out to others and earn a little stake money so. Then again, it was often quicker and easier to set upon and rob some traveller in an out-of-the-way location and simply take his money and belongings. Saddler would have taken oath that this was what Stock and his friend were aiming for here.

Imperceptibly, he took a firmer grip on the rifle tucked beneath his arm and brought his left hand across his body, ready to grasp the fore-end, should need arise.

Stock's friend Joe still had his eyes fixed on Saddler.

'You ain't told us all yet,' he said. 'What you have in the back o' your cart?'

Stock said, in a reasonable tone, 'We only want a small part of your goods, Saddler,' then, seeing his partner's hand moving towards the holster at his hip, he cried, 'No, Joe, that ain't needed!'

But it was too late now, because the man he had introduced as Joe Collins had grown tired of a heap of talking and just wanted whatever Saddler was carrying in his wagon. He went for his pistol, and at the same instant Saddler brought up his rifle and fired at him. Then he dropped the rifle and pulled the pistol from his own belt and fired at Abraham Stock, who had not even gone for his gun. Saddler didn't know if he had hit the man called Joe, but that individual had seemingly had enough anyway, because he spurred his horse on and galloped off. Saddler didn't fire after him.

Stock had fallen from his horse and was lying stunned on the ground. His horse had skittered off, spooked by the gunfire and was standing off about forty feet from her owner. A dark stain was spreading across Stock's shirt, just beneath the ribs, and he was panting for breath. Saddler squatted down to see if there was anything he could do for the man he had shot.

'You shouldn't o' jumped me, Stock,' he said. 'You know it wasn't the smart move.'

'We was desperate,' said the other. 'We hadn't ate for nearly two days. Had to do somethin'.'

'Something, yes, but not robbing me. You might o' knowed it would turn out like this.'

The wounded man closed his eyes and his breathing became more rapid and shallow. Then he opened his eyes again and, looking over Saddler's shoulder, said, 'Hey, little lady.'

Saddler looked round and found that Abigail had left the wagon and was standing behind him, gazing down at the dying man.

'Get along back to the wagon,' he told her roughly. 'This ain't a sight for little girls!'

'Let her be, Saddler,' said Stock faintly. 'She looks a nice little thing.'

'I'm sorry that you have been shot,' said the child in her high, clear voice. 'But from what I saw, your friend brought it on. He went for his gun.'

Stock coughed and a little blood escaped from his mouth. 'Joe always was hasty,' he said. 'It's how we lost our money. But that don't seem to matter overmuch now.' He closed his eyes again and didn't reopen them. As Saddler and Abigail watched, his breathing stopped and he died.

'Next time I tell you to do something, you do it,' said Saddler. He stood up and looked at Abigail, who in turn was looking down at Stock. 'You hear what I tell you, child?'

'He doesn't look like a bad man,' observed Abigail.

'That's a lot of nonsense,' said Saddler brusquely. 'You can't tell by looking at a man's face whether he's good or bad or will play you false. It's what he does that makes him what he is, not having a nice smile, or white, even teeth.'

'Was he bad?' asked Abigail.

'No, I wouldn't say so. He was desperate and that can drive men into evil ways. I rode with him once and he played fair with me. I'm sorry I shot him, but there it is.'

3

Saddler flat refused to bury the man he had killed, on the grounds that the sooner they were moving the sooner they would reach Kansas and be able to find Abigail's grandfather. He consented to the child saying a prayer over Stock's corpse, but refused to join in, even to the extent of merely saying 'Amen' at the end of the prayer.

Once they were on the move again, Saddler said, 'I don't rightly know how we're going to manage this. I have only a quarter or so in cash money and no chance of gettin' more for now.'

To Saddler's surprise, Abigail said, 'I have some money, if it would help.'

'The hell you do! How much?'

'My father gave my mother two gold coins to sew into my bodice.'

'You kept that quiet.'

'My father said that they were for emergencies.'

'Well,' said Saddler, 'I don't know what you'd call this, other than an emergency. We are apt to go hungry and thirsty without money.'

Abigail didn't speak for a minute or so and then said, 'I mind you are right. If you let me have a knife, I will unpick the threads and remove the coins.'

Reaching behind him, Saddler pulled out the knife which he kept in a sheath at the back of his belt. He handed it to Abigail, who said, 'I must get in back of the wagon and take off my dress. Don't look.'

He kept the wagon moving along at a steady pace, while the girl clambered from her seat and got into the back of the cart.

It was a funny thing about Abraham Stock. Saddler had known him vaguely for a couple of years and then last year he had ridden with Stock and a few others in a raid on a stage. That had gone off as smooth as you like, with nobody killed and not a single shot fired. Stock had struck him as an amiable enough fellow, if not overly endowed with brains, and Saddler regretted that he had ended up killing the man. Still and all, once people began trying to rob him, it stood to reason that things would get ugly. He had not gone looking for trouble today and so Stock's blood was upon his own head; leastways, that was how Saddler saw the case.

Abigail scrambled back into the seat next to him and shyly offered Saddler the two coins which she had unpicked from her clothing. He examined them curiously.

'These are Baldwin horseman ten dollar pieces,' he exclaimed in surprise. 'They made 'em in California 'fore the war.'

'Would you like to look after them?' asked the girl.

'I'll take care of them, Abigail,' he told her. 'I think these should keep us goin' for a bit. I might even be able to get rid of those crates back there, with luck, which means that we wouldn't need to break into these. We'll see.'

None of the roads passing through the Indian territories were in a particularly good state of repair and the one along which they were currently travelling was no exception. It was perhaps being overly generous to dignify any of the tracks which ran through the district with the name 'road', they being more in the nature of what would be termed dirt tracks anywhere else.

This track led north, in the general direction of Kansas. Even under ideal circumstances and with no delays, it might take a week to reach the border and the Lord knew how much longer after that to track down Abigail's family. Still, Ben Saddler was a man who, once having taken on a task, would stick at it to the bitter end.

'What will we do about food this evening?' asked the girl.

'There's a place some miles north of here, as would fit the bill there,' said

Saddler. 'It's an outpost of the Indian Bureau and some other buildings. There's a store and suchlike. Happen we'll be able to get vittles there. Jackrabbit's all well and good, but we don't want to be eating nothing but for a week.'

'Do you think there will be a bed there for us?'

Saddler gave the child an amused look. 'Lord,' he said, 'I couldn't say. Like as not there'll be nothing o' the kind.'

They travelled for a space in silence and then Abigail said, 'Where do you live? Don't you have some home of your own?'

'Not since I left the army I haven't. I've lived hither and thither, but not more than two or three months in one spot.'

'Don't you feel you'd like to have a house of your own?' asked Abigail, a little wistfully. 'It must be awful nice.'

'From what you say,' replied Saddler, 'you been livin' the same way, meaning that you moved here and there.'

It seemed to Saddler that he and Abigail were getting on quite sociably and that she was losing somewhat of her aloofness with him. The afternoon wore on to early evening before they reached the little hamlet that clustered around the office of the Indian Bureau.

In theory, at least, the Indian territories were like an independent nation, or more precisely a confederation of five nations, a quite different category from the reservations. In reality though, Washington was determined to keep a watch on the area and so the federal government made sure that they had their agents scattered here and there so that they could keep a finger on the pulse, as it were.

The place where Saddler was heading was on the western fringes of the Chickasaw Nation. The territories were divided up into what were nominally the nations of the five civilized tribes; Cherokee, Chickasaw, Choctaw, Creek and Seminole. The Chickasaw nation was on the edge of the Indian Territory, right next to the stretch of country whose citizens hoped one day to achieve statehood as Oklahoma.

Saddler and his young companion reached the crest of the high ground overlooking the Chickasaw office of the Indian Bureau and he at once received a shock. There were the rambling wood and stone buildings of the Indian Bureau and the other, smaller buildings that had grown up alongside it, as though sheltering in its lee. But when last he had passed this way there had not been an encampment of US cavalry, with rows of tents pitched right by the little hamlet. Saddler pulled up and rubbed his chin thoughtfully.

'What's up?' said Abigail. 'Why have you stopped?'

'This ain't good, child. Not good at all.'

'Why? Those soldiers won't trouble us, will they?'

'I hope not,' said Saddler, slowly. 'But I aimed just to pass through here an'' pick up one or two things without drawin' overmuch attention to us.'

'Does that mean we are not going down there?'

'Hush now,' he said, 'and let me think.'

Saddler counted the tents and did a rough calculation. By his reckoning there was maybe half a company of soldiers camped out next to the bureau offices: say fifty men or so. They weren't after him, that was for sure. It was most likely some raid by a party of Indians that they had been called in to deal with. The more he thought about it, the more he came to the conclusion that this might not be so bad after all. He might even be able to unload that whiskey in back of his wagon.

Then it came to him that he could maybe get shot of the wagon too. It was a broken-down old rattletrap anyway and like to fall to pieces by itself if he forced it too hard along some of the tracks in these parts. He could see if anybody would trade it for a little pony that Abigail could ride. It would not be hard to sell such a beast once they hit Kansas and he couldn't see that he would lose on the deal.

Saddler turned to Abigail and asked, 'Can you ride?'

'Yes, I had my own pony for a spell.'

'I have it in mind to get rid of this cart, so we can both ride. We'd make faster time so.'

'What about all those boxes in the back?'

'I aim to dispose of 'em. Let's go down and see what's brewin'. Listen up, though. I don't want you drawin' no attention to yourself or anything. Is that clear?'

'I'm not given to showing off and suchlike,' said Abigail, a little affronted.

'I only meant that we're to be inconspicuous and blend in. You get me?'

Ranged along the dusty track which passed for the main street of the area, were a blacksmith's and livery stable, a couple of stores, a poky eating house and a chapel. The proprietors of these enterprises lived over the premises and their customers were passing travellers, rather than folk actually living in the neighbourhood. Dominating the 'street' was the impressive bulk of the Indian Bureau. It was built partly of stone and had a more solid and substantial look about it than the other buildings.

As they drove along, Saddler explained to Abigail how things stood.

'The Chickasaw sided with us in the late war,' he told her. 'That's to say, they joined with the Confederacy. Which irked the Unionists, and after the war ended they took a heap of the Chickasaws' land to punish 'em. So the Indians hereabouts ain't none too fond of Uncle Sam, to put it mildly.'

'Did you fight in the war?'

'From beginning to end,' he said proudly. 'Joined up the day we shelled those rascals out o' Fort Sumner an' I was with Lee when he surrendered at Appomattox.'

'My family were abolitionists. I

suppose you owned slaves?'

'Me? No, we were dirt-poor. I never owned a slave in my life. You think I look like some rich plantation owner?'

They parked up the wagon and Saddler unhitched his horse and took her over to the livery stable. Abigail stood watching for a while, but didn't stay to listen to the conversation that Saddler had with the owner of that place. By the time they had finished talking and the conversation had ended with the two men shaking hands, she had wandered off.

Not wishing to spend one of Abigail's gold pieces, Saddler had agreed to pay in whiskey for what he wanted, which suited the owner right well. The territories were technically 'dry' and although it was possible to buy liquor, there was a high premium on it. This was, of course, why Saddler had thought it worthwhile bringing crates of whiskey into the district. The owner of the livery stable had an interest in the eating house too, and was keen to do business with Saddler over the whiskey. With a heap of cavalrymen camped near by, there was a stiff demand for intoxicating liquor.

After they had shaken on the deal Saddler turned, only to find that Abigail was no longer at his side. He heard raised voices across the street and when he looked, found to his dismay that the girl was at the centre of some kind of dispute. Cursing silently, he went over to see what was happening.

While Saddler was dickering with the man from the livery stable, Abigail walked over to where a young Indian boy, about the same age as her, was selling snacks to the soldiers. He had a leather bag slung over his shoulder, which contained little parcels of cold, spicy meat wrapped in cornpone. As she watched, Abigail saw to her disgust that one of the soldiers snatched the bag from the boy and was evidently intent on making off with his stock of food without paying a cent.

The Indian boy was almost in tears,

and quite unable to tackle the man who had taken his wares from him, and who towered above him like a giant. A group of a dozen or so soldiers were laughing and jeering at the boy's fruitless attempts to regain his bag. She went up to the man and said loudly,

'You are a coward. You would not dare do that to a grown man.'

The spectators to the scene stopped laughing and watched to see what would happen next. The man who had taken the bag from the Indian said, 'You run along, little britches and tend to your own affairs.'

'This is my affair,' said Abigail hotly, 'You are a thief and a bully. You think I will turn my eyes from that? I will not. Give that bag back to its owner at once.'

The Indian had stopped grabbing at his bag and was looking in amazement at the little girl who stood there reproving a grown man in this way. The other men who had been egging on their comrade had also fallen silent.

'Did you hear what I said?' asked the girl. 'Give him back his property.'

The hulking bully who had snatched away the boy's bag made as if to strike at Abigail. The blow was not given in earnest and was most likely only a feint, intended to make her jump back, but if so, his hand did not have the opportunity to make contact with the child. As he made as though to deliver a backhanded cuff to this irritating little girl, the soldier's arm was seized from behind in a vicelike grip. A bony hand, backed by tough sinews and an indomitable will, grasped his arm painfully, just above the elbow. At the same moment, a man behind him said,

'You mind what you're about there. I wouldn't lay a finger on that child, were I you.'

The man holding the Indian's bag tried to jerk his arm free, but it might as well have been caught in a gin-trap. Saddler said to the girl, 'What's to do?'

'That man stole the bag of food from the Indian boy. He was hawking snacks round and that man just took his bag from him.'

The cavalrymen who had been amused to see a little girl berating their brother in arms were considerably less tolerant of a grown man catching hold of one of them. There were murmurs of discontent, which Saddler took to be indicative of the first stirrings of trouble. He asked the man whose arm he was still holding,

'Is that true, what she says? Did you take that there bag from the boy?'

'What's it to you?' asked the man angrily. 'You best let ago of my arm there.'

Saddler released the fellow's arm and stepped back at once.

'It's this to me,' he said. 'I can't abide bullies. If you took that from the boy, you can just hand it back and then if'n you feel like doin' some bullying, try your luck on me. If you ain't afeared to get crosswise to a grown man, that is.'

The man in front of him tossed the bag to the ground, whereupon the boy eagerly snatched it up and hugged it to his chest. He didn't leave though, but stood and waited to see how matters would develop. The fistfight that everybody expected, never had a chance to begin, because just then their officer, a fresh-faced young captain, came striding towards the group and demanded to know what the Sam Hill was going on.

None of the soldiers seemed keen to explain the matter and Saddler was content to let things rest. It was Abigail who piped up,

'One of your men stole something from that boy and my friend here made him give it back.'

The young captain turned to Saddler and asked, 'That right?'

'Pretty well. Looked like looting to me, which is to say stealing from the civilian population. We shot men for that during the war.'

'I don't need instruction in military law,' said the officer curtly. 'You men fall in and follow me now.'

When once the soldiers had left, Saddler turned to Abigail and said, 'Didn't you hear when I told you we wanted to be inconspicuous here? Why'd you go roamin' off like that?'

'I don't like bullies. That food was like as not all this boy has and he needs to make money by selling it. It was wicked to try and steal it.'

The Indian boy was still standing there, staring at them, so Saddler said, 'Alright son, you can run along now.'

'Thank you,' said the boy. 'Thank you.' He smiled at Abigail and then left them. Saddler was gazing thoughtfully after him. He said,

'Something's not right here. That boy ain't a Chickasaw. He's Chiricahua. What's he doin' in this here town?'

'How do you know he's a chiri — what you said?' asked Abigail.

'His people mark their sons as babies, make little scars on their cheeks. I wonder the Chickasaw put up with a Chiricahua Apache working in this place. Unless . . . '

'Unless what?'

'Never mind. We've business to attend to.'

'What do you mean?'

'I mean I've a buyer for my wares and've engaged to buy a pony for you to ride. We'll need a blanket and one or two other things, maybe some food. I'll warrant you're hungry this moment?'

'Maybe a little.'

'How if I left you in yon' eating house and went about my business,' Saddler said, 'you'd be bored silly by trailin' round after me.'

There were only two customers in the eating house, both of them soldiers. Saddler ordered food for Abigail and when she was seated at a table, told her, 'You are not to set foot from this place while I'm gone. You mark what I say?'

'Of course I won't. I will sit here until you return.'

He looked at her for a moment and then added, 'There's trouble in the wind, Abigail. I want to know where you are, just in case.'

'In case of what?'

'I don't rightly know. Just in case.'

Business of this nature, selling whiskey, bargaining over horseflesh and so on, were meat and drink to Ben Saddler. In the usual way of things he would have been as casual and relaxed as a baby in a crib as he went about such matters but, as it was, he could not shake off the feeling of foreboding. Something bad was going to happen. He felt it in his bones and the sooner he had converted his whiskey into cash money, the easier he would be in his mind.

The liquor fetched more than he had figured it would, on account of all the soldiers thereabouts who were gasping for a drink. He did not make as much as he would have done by selling to Indians, but he had made a tidy profit, nevertheless. The man at the livery stable had sneered at the wagon, but Saddler could see that he wanted it really. After some tough bartering, Saddler had, by throwing in a couple of bottles of whiskey too, exchanged it for a little pony that would suit Abigail. After picking up an extra blanket, buying a little food for the journey and one or two other things, he felt that they were pretty well fixed up. He headed back to the eating house.

As he was about to enter the place where he had left Abigail, it suddenly struck Saddler that there was one small matter which he had altogether overlooked and that was clothes for the child. She surely could not ride the trail on horseback wearing that long, black dress of hers! The store across the way sold work clothes and such, so he doubled back and went into it. Appearing here with a little girl and then kitting her out to dress like a boy would surely draw attention and invite unwanted questions, so Saddler decided simply to buy the things without her being present.

The storekeeper didn't seem to find anything remarkable about a man buying clothes for a young fellow who wasn't with him. Saddler indicated roughly the height and build of his ficticious nephew and bought a pair of pants and a work shirt. Then he went back to the eating house and rejoined Abigail.

'You were a long time,' said Abigail. 'I thought something had happened to you.'

'No,' said Saddler, 'I'm fine. I'll have some food myself and then we will see what's next.'

After he had eaten his fill, the two of them walked out into the street. It was a bright, sunny evening, but Saddler felt a chill in the air. He announced abruptly, 'Something's wrong. We gotta leave, right now.'

'Why?' said Abigail. 'What's the matter?'

'You ever been outside during a storm and felt the hairs prickle on the back of your neck, because you know the lightning's about to strike?'

'Not that I recall,' said the child practically. 'We generally stayed indoors when it was raining.'

Saddler looked round the little group of buildings, cast an eye round the cavalry encampment, and then shook his head.

'I'm telling you now, something's not right. We're goin' to collect those horses and make tracks.'

'I thought we were staying here for the night?'

'Not any more we ain't,' said Saddler and there was no more to be said on the subject. He had evidently made up his mind.

4

Abigail cavilled a little at the notion of changing her clothes in the hayloft at the livery stable, but Saddler was inflexible and determined about the whole thing. With considerable bad grace, she finally went along with the scheme.

Towering above the little settlement was a huge, sandstone bluff; part of a massif that stretched north as far as the Cimarron river. A path twisted and turned up into the mountains, and along this Saddler and Abigail made their way up into the hills.

'It feels strange to be wearing pants,' said Abigail. 'They are not so comfortable as a dress.'

'A sight easier for ridin', though,' replied Saddler. 'You couldn't straddle that pony wearing a dress.'

'That's true. What are you afraid of?

Why did we have to leave that place so suddenly?'

'I don't rightly know, Abigail. Sometimes I get a feeling and it's like I'm being warned of danger. I felt so when I rode into the little wood where I found you.'

'You mean what is called a premonition?'

'I don't know the word. It's like a tingling. I had it during the war, an' each and every time it was telling me o' some threat I hadn't known of. I ain't about to disregard that feeling.'

The two of them rode on until they reached the top of the steep slope and could see the plain laid out before them to the south. The buildings around the Indian Bureau looked like a child's toys from this height. Saddler dismounted and told the child to do the same. Then the two of them removed the saddles from his horse and the pony. There was a little coarse grass on the plateau which lay behind the bluff and Saddler said that it would be all right to let the beasts graze a little. He arranged their things behind a boulder, which gave shelter from the wind. Seated there, they could not be seen from below and yet had a good view of the Indian Bureau and the surrounding area.

They each ate an apple from their stores, as they gazed down at the scene below. So used had he grown to the little girl's eerily self-possessed ways, that Saddler had got into the way of thinking of her almost as a grown-up person, rather than a child. So it was that when he saw her shoulders shaking up and down as she looked out across the country with her back to him, Saddler thought that she might have something stuck in her throat.

'You all right there?' he asked.

She didn't reply and he was scared that she was choking on a piece of apple and so reached forward to touch her shoulder. Then Abigail turned to face him and he was horrified to see that she was weeping openly.

Through her tears, the child said, 'I

miss my ma and pa. I miss them so much. I know it's wrong to grieve for them, but I can't help it.'

Now Saddler had never been much of a one for handling other folk's emotions, and for a second or two he was lost for words. Then it struck him that no words of his would help the poor little thing and that what she chiefly needed was comforting. He put his arm around her and the girl buried her face in his shoulder and cried hopelessly for some little while. As she did so, Saddler limited himself to making soothing noises and saying things such as, 'There, there' and 'Everything will be all right'.

At length, the little girl stopped sobbing and looked up at Saddler. She said, 'You must think me a regular baby to carry on so.'

'Nothing of the kind. It's a sight more natural than keepin' your feelings hidden away inside. I'm only sorry I can't do anything for you, child.'

Abigail looked at him in surprise.

'Oh, but you have,' she said. 'I cannot think that anybody could have been kinder to me.'

'Lord,' said Saddler, embarrassed. 'I ain't in that mould at all. It's some good long time while since anybody told me I was kind.'

'You pretend not to be. You are the kindest person I ever met.'

Saddler looked vaguely discomfited, as though he had been caught out cheating at cards. 'Don't speak so,' he said. 'It wouldn't do my reputation any good if folks got to hear of it. People'd take advantage of me.'

'I know I've been a nuisance to you. Really, why have you taken all this trouble to help me?'

He said nothing for a few seconds and Abigail thought that he was annoyed with her for pressing the point.

Then Saddler said, 'It's like this. When I was just your age, I was cruelly used by some of the men in the orphans' asylum.'

'You mean they beat you?'

'That too. But there was worse. Beastly things such as I wouldn't like to tell of. I prayed for help, I wished some grown-up would come to my aid. Nobody ever did and I had to get through it alone. When I found you, Abigail, I knew I had to help you as best I was able. That's all.' From the plain beneath them, came the sharp, clear note of a bugle. Saddler said, 'Hallo, what's to do?'

They looked down at the hamlet and saw that the cavalry were mounted up and looked to be ready to move out. It was twilight and the sun had sunk right below the horizon. Abigail said, 'They're leaving.'

'Not for good. See now, they left their tents up. They're off on a sortie. Like as not, they heard word of some Chickasaw raiding party in the area and are going after 'em.'

As the man and child watched, the troop of soldiers moved off, heading east into the heart of the Chickasaw nation. Everything looked as peaceful and quiet as could be after they left and Saddler suggested that Abigail wrap herself up in a blanket and try to get some sleep. For his own part, he purposed to sit for a space, gazing south and west. The girl had the impression that he was waiting for something or expecting trouble, but if so he kept his own counsel.

It was pitch dark when Abigail awoke. At least, it was the middle of a moonless night, and so there should have been no light at all. For a moment she wondered where she was and then recollected that they had climbed the bluff overlooking the hamlet. She wondered what had woken her and then realized that there was a source of light which was not the moon or stars. It was a ruddy, flickering glow and it came from below and not from the sky above. There was something else as well; the faint sound of shouting, triumphant voices. Saddler was sitting by the boulder, peering intently down towards the Indian Bureau.

'What it is?' she asked, 'What's happening?'

'It's nothing to fret about. Go back to sleep now.'

Abigail shrugged off the blanket and went over to join him.

He said, 'Keep down. Don't make a profile against the sky.'

'What's going on?'

'Yon settlement is being attacked. Those horse soldiers was lured away on a snipe hunt and now the Indians are destroying the place.'

The buildings were all alight, which accounted for the red glow she had seen. By the light of the flames, Abigail could see shadowy forms riding round the blazing stores, eating house and livery stable. The offices of the Indian Bureau alone did not seem to be burning, and as she watched she became aware of the crack of rifle fire.

'How did it happen?' she asked Saddler.

'That's no mystery,' he told her. 'Once those soldier boys were a two- or three-hour ride from here a bunch of warriors rode down and torched the place. I guess the men in the Indian Bureau are holding them off, but it won't be long before they're done for as well.'

'Can't we do anything to help them?'

Saddler sighed and said, 'Abigail, it's one of those times when you got to sit tight. I have to watch, to see how it ends. There's no need for you to do so. Why don't you go back to sleep?'

'No, I reckon I'll watch too.'

The lower half of the complex of buildings which made up the offices of the Indian Bureau was constructed of stone. It must have proved impossible so far for the Indians to set fire to it. All the other structures that made up the settlement were entirely wood and so it had probably only been a matter of piling brushwood up against the side of them and then kindling it. As they watched there were flashes from the windows of the Indian Bureau, followed a second or two later by the sound of shots.

'They're game enough, those men from the bureau,' said Saddler, 'but it'll do 'em no good.' He was proved right a few minutes later when the first flickering flames could be see licking the wooden, upper storeys of the building. 'I'll warrant they been splashing lamp oil about. Dry summer, it's been; that wood'll go up like a tinderbox.'

In half an hour it was a straight choice for the men and women in the burning offices: to remain within and burn to death or to bolt and hope for mercy from the Indians besieging the place. Bright rectangles of light appeared as doors opened and figures were framed in the openings. There were whoops of delight from the Indians as they set to massacring those who surrendered. Abigail couldn't bear to watch; she turned her back and huddled up in the blanket, trying to block her ears to the cries of those being killed. She dozed off again and when next she opened her eyes it was dawn.

Saddler was sitting in just exactly the same position as he had been during the night, and as far as she could gauge he had not moved at all. He was still staring down intently at the scene below them. Abigail yawned and without turning round, Saddler said,

'Don't you stand up or show yourself against the sky. You want to come over here, then crawl on your hands and knees.'

As Abigail wriggled over to where the man sat she became aware of the tantalizing smell of roast meat.

'Are they having a barbecue down there?' she asked and then a dreadful thought struck her. 'That smell. It's not . . . not *people?*'

'It is,' said Saddler grimly. 'What d'you expect when a bunch of wooden buildings burn with everybody in them?'

The smell of burnt meat mingled in the morning air with the fragrance of wood smoke and Abigail felt suddenly sick. She scrabbled across the ground to throw up some distance away.

Saddler called over, 'We need to move from here soon. You want any breakfast?'

His matter-of-fact manner calmed her and she consented to share some bread and cheese. As they ate, she asked,

'Will we carry on the same, now this has happened?'

'No. The sooner we get clear o' the Chickasaw nation the better. They're right vexed with the white man just now. I ain't about to head north from here. We'll make north-east and work our way into the Choctaw territory.'

'Was it the Chickasaw who killed all those folks last night?'

'No, it weren't. I knew when I saw that Chiricahua boy yesterday that something was amiss. I'll take oath that those braves last night were Chiricahua Apaches. The Chickasaws led the cavalry away on a mad chase and then once they were out o' the way, the Chiricahuas rode in. It was neatly done, I'll allow.'

'Neatly done? How can you speak so about a heap of murders?'

Saddler said nothing for a spell and then observed,

'Nobody asked us to come here and take their land. What they're doing is no worse than what we all did in the War between the States. They just defending themselves.'

There was no sign of life in the burnt out buildings around the Indian Bureau. Whatever had lured the cavalry away, they had not yet returned. They were in for something of a shock when they did, because the Indians had made sure to burn all their tents and steal any stores left behind. The raid had, as Saddler remarked, been very neatly done.

The horses had not wandered far and it did not take long to tack them up and make ready to break camp. Saddler wanted them to take a trail leading down from the plateau on which they were currently situated and which led east and then north, in the general direction of the Choctaw nation. Not knowing enough about the geography of the area to be able to offer an intelligent comment about this plan Abigail chose to remain silent.

Saddler's horse seemed a good deal happier being ridden than it had done being harnessed up and expected to draw a cart behind it. It was ready and raring to go. The pony which he had acquired for Abigail was a little slower and lacked the zip of the larger animal, but suited her well enough. Although, as she had told Saddler, she had once owned a pony of her own, she was but an indifferent rider and the pony, who sensed this, took full advantage of her inexperience, showing a tendency to stop and graze every few seconds.

The man and his young companion made their way down the path leading off the mountains and Saddler was congratulating himself on having made the smart choice when, up ahead, he saw a sight which filled him with horror. A war party of braves was heading straight towards them. They were painted up and armed to the teeth and it could hardly be doubted that these were the very men who had made such short work of the nearby settlement not twelve hours since. Saddler reined in and desired Abigail to do the same, although her pony had stopped as soon as his horse had halted.

'Are these men looking for trouble, would you say?' asked Abigail nervously. Saddler hadn't the heart to give her an honest answer, saying instead:

'Let's see what they have to say.'

He surreptitiously loosened the pistol tucked in his belt. If it looked as though these boys meant mischief towards them, then he had no intention of allowing the little girl to be captured alive and treated barbarously. Better by far that he put an end to her life, than that he leave her at the mercy of such men. He had seen at first hand the way that the Apache treated their female prisoners.

There were perhaps forty or more men in the band, which was fast bearing down upon them. To bring together such a large war party argued for careful planning; last night's activity was obviously not a spur-of-the-moment attack. The Chickasaw and Chiricahua had seemingly buried the hatchet over their own long-standing differences and joined together to fight the common foe.

Mentally, Ben Saddler cursed the greedy men who were apparently determined to drive the Red Man from the rest of his land. Even when the Indians had been confined to reservations and this supposedly 'Indian' territory, still they could not forbear to steal even the portions of land remaining to the Indians. No wonder they were on the war path!

Things did not look at all promising as the heavily armed band drew near and then surrounded the two travellers. Saddler made no hostile move, but was very ready for the attack. He really could not see how he and the child were likely to be spared. It was then that he received a great surprise, when the young boy whom he and Abigail had stood up for the previous day pushed his little pony through the ranks of warriors and began first by talking excitedly and then shouting urgently. The men nearest to him turned and listened gravely to what he was saying and then, without a word, the riders in front of Saddler and Abigail parted, leaving a clear path forward for the two white people. The boy, who really could not have been any older than Abigail, smiled at them and said, as he had done the day before, 'Thank you!'

Hardly daring to believe their luck, Saddler led the way through the Apache braves, none of whom made any attempt to molest him or Abigail.

When they were clear of the Chiricahua, Saddler breathed a sigh of relief. He realized that he was running with sweat. He had been certain sure that those boys had had it in mind to kill him and then take the child away for Lord knows what horrors. Abigail, being a child, had not perhaps fully understood the danger in which they had been, although she looked a little white and shaky. 'Well, Mr Saddler,' she said, 'we surely cast our bread upon the waters that time!'

'Hey? What's that you say?' he enquired.

'It says in the Bible that if you cast your bread upon the waters, it will return to you tenfold. Meaning that acts of charity will bring you a reward. Helping that boy yesterday has saved our lives, don't you see?'

'That's one way of viewin' the case,' said Saddler gruffly. 'That was the hell of a fix we was in. I didn't think we'd make it out of there.'

'Oh, something always turns up,' said the girl cheerfully, 'You must never despair, you know.'

As far as Saddler knew the Choctaws had no sort of reason to feel aggrieved with white folk just at that present moment, leastways, no more reason than usual. At any rate they had not just had another chunk of their land stolen away from them, the way that the Chickasaw had. That being so, the two of them might be a little safer in their territory, although of course, you could never be certain sure.

Abigail was disposed to chatter while they rode, which Saddler found pleasant. Her crying yesterday looked to him to have unloosed something within her and she was a mite more open than she had been.

'Don't you ever wish that you had a little house, all of your own?' she asked wistfully. 'It must be so nice to stay in just the one spot for years at a time. Don't you feel the same way?'

Saddler turned the question over in his mind, before replying. At length, he said,

'Now that you set the case out so, I won't say as I wouldn't like that. I been a roaming type, what some call a rolling stone. I ain't never put down roots.'

'Did you never marry?' asked Abigail and then blushed, saying hastily, 'What a thing to say. I'm sorry.'

He chuckled. 'That's nothing. No, I never married, leastways, not yet I ain't. There's time enough; I'm not all that old. Had one or two sweethearts, but nothin' ever came of it.'

They rode on for the day, seeing only a very few other travellers, all of them Indians. None of these others appeared to want to talk or have any dealings with them, which was just fine by Saddler.

They stopped every couple of hours so that Abigail could stretch her legs. The famous pony, of which she had made mention, turned out to have been only in her possession for three months and that when she was nine. She hadn't ridden much since then and it was an uncomfortable experience for her.

After they had halted for the third or fourth time, she said, 'I have a terrible pain in my . . . that is to say in a certain part of my body.'

Saddler laughed at this, saying, 'You will get used to it in time. It's quicker than driving that wagon.'

By evening they had, according to Saddler's calculations, entered the Choctaw territory. There was no reason to fear most of the people living in this part of the territories, although of course, like anywhere else, there were bad people. A lot of his trading in recent months had been with the Choctaw, and Saddler had always found them to be honest in their dealings, although exceedingly shrewd and canny bargainers. Even so, there was no percentage in taking unnecessary chances, and so Saddler insisted that they make their camp that night in some woods. He wanted to be off the road and out view.

Despite his caution, Saddler could see no cause to forbid the lighting of a little cooking fire. Apart from food, he had a desperate craving for coffee. After they had eaten and drunk their fill, the two of them stretched out and relaxed.

Abigail said, 'You are sure that we will be safe here tonight?'

'No, I ain't *sure*. There's no such thing in this world. I mind though that we are no more at risk than we would be in the average town. The Indians in these parts are not bloodthirsty savages. They're just folks like you an' me. I think we will be fine here.'

As it happened, Ben Saddler could hardly have been more wrong about that, but to be fair to him, the danger that found them there the next morning could not have been foreseen. Still and all, Abigail came closer to losing her life in that little wood than at any other point in their journey to Kansas.

5

Abigail was sound asleep as the sun rose the next day. Slowly though, she was roused to consciousness by a strange sensation: as if somebody was tickling her nose. At first she moved her hand up in her sleep, to brush away whatever it was causing the sensation. It stopped for a little and then there it was again, the lightest of touches, only this time accompanied by a slight noise.

Eventually, she came to and opened her eyes; whereupon she almost screamed out loud. There, just a few inches from her face, a pair of twinkling brown eyes were regarding her curiously. Abigail jerked back in fear and then saw that the owner of the eyes was a bear cub that wanted to play. As she watched it, it leaned forward and licked her nose, which was probably what had woken her up.

The bear cub was so adorable and cuddly that Abigail could not resist throwing off her blanket and sitting up. The cub jumped back in alarm when she did so and waited six feet away, as though making sure that there was no danger. Abigail stood up and walked over to the little bear and reached out a hand tentatively. To her delight, she found that the cub was happy for her to scratch his head and fondle his ears, as though he were a cat or a puppy. Then he jumped back again and moved further off. She followed him.

Saddler was snoring lightly while all this was going on. He had barely slept a wink on the night of the Apache attack and had been dog tired when he closed his eyes the previous night. As he slept, Abigail followed the bear cub further into the woods. Her eyes were shining with pleasure, and for the first time since the death of her parents she was smiling happily. It did not for a moment occur to her that she might be in any danger.

The bear led her to a little clearing, where the grass and undergrowth seemed to have been trampled down or crushed. The significance of this escaped her. She was so busy playing with the bear cub that she didn't even hear the return of the creature's mother, who had been out foraging for food. When it saw what it assumed was a predator pursuing its only cub, the she-bear gave a mighty roar and reared up on its hind legs. Abigail turned round and almost fainted in terror at the frightful sight of a fully grown black bear which was about to attack her.

The protracted snarl of the angry bear jolted Saddler from his slumbers. He knew at once what the sound meant and, on seeing that Abigail was not lying next to him, he leaped to his feet.

Abigail was sprightly and young and that is what saved her life. The huge creature swung a paw at what she perceived to be the threat to her offspring. Had those razor sharp claws caught Abigail it would all have been up with her. She jumped back though, seeing what the bear was about to do. Just at that same instant Ben Saddler came running into the glade. He commenced to roar and shout at the mother bear in an effort to draw her attention away from Abigail. The bear turned round and for a fraction of a second Saddler's life hung in the balance. Then, obeying some imperative of her own, the great beast lowered her bulk back on to all four of her paws and, shepherding her cub before her, ambled away into the forest.

'Did she hurt you?' Saddler asked.

'No, I moved back in time.'

'What in the hell were you thinking of, wandering off in that wise? You lost your senses or what?'

Hearing his cross voice, coming so soon after such a terrible scare, Abigail promptly burst into tears. Saddler felt remorseful for scolding her and at once went over to the child and put his arms round her.

'There, there,' he said, 'don't take on

so. I was worried for you is all.'

Later on, as they breakfasted, Saddler told her about black bears.

'Thing with those bears is that you can often scare them away by shouting and waving your arms at 'em. They don't want to fight. Not like grizzlies, mind. Shout at one o' them and they're apt to rip your head clean off your shoulders.'

Abigail had recovered from her fright and said, 'The cub was awful cute. I felt like I could have cuddled it.'

'Which,' observed Saddler, 'is how you damn near got yourself killed.'

When they started out that morning, Saddler said, 'By late afternoon we should be at a little town called Fort Renown.'

'Is it an Indian town or do white folks live there?'

'Just white folks. It's an old army fort and after the end of the war, a bunch o' settlers moved in there to stake claim to some land in the territories. They'd no business doing it, but the Choctaw weren't versed in law and so they couldn't stop 'em.'

'Didn't the Indians try to fight them?' asked Abigail.

'No, they traded with 'em. Anyways, more people moved in until this fort has become a little white town, stuck right plumb-bang in the heart of the Choctaw nation.'

'Why are we going there?'

'Two reasons. First off, is where it's on our way. Second is that you could do with sleeping in a bed for a night or two. There's some kind of lodging house at Fort Renown. We'll find you a bed for the night.'

Abigail found the ride a lot easier that day, notwithstanding the fact that she was still mighty sore from the previous day. As they travelled, Saddler gave her various hints and tips about controlling her mount, with the result that by the time they reached Fort Renown at about four that afternoon, she was able to keep the pony moving pretty well, despite his natural inclinations to laziness and sloth.

Fort Renown was a wooden stockade type fort which had been erected in somewhat of a hurry in the first few months of the war. It had originally consisted of little more than walls of whittled tree trunks, sharpened at the top and lined up side by side. There were watch-towers at each corner, and to begin with the soldiers quartered there had lived in tents, pitched inside the stockade. Gradually other buildings had been thrown up inside; a barracks, canteen, armoury and so on.

After the war had ended some settlers who did not feel inclined to join in land rushes heard about the abandoned forts in the Indian Territories and decided that there would be less competition for land and resources in such locations. This led to the founding of a half-dozen little towns, each surrounded by scatterings of farms. The whole thing was a flagrant violation of the treaties made with the five civilized tribes but, since the government in Washington was already breaking those same treaties, nobody felt inclined to stop these illegal settlers from drifting into the area.

The forts provided the focal point for the white settlers, who had in general as little to do with the Indians as they were able. There were stores, blacksmiths, saloons, brothels, churches and everything else that civilized people might require within the walls of the old stockades. There was no official law and so vigilance committees sprang up to administer beatings and the occasional hanging to keep the rougher elements in check.

There were great wooden gates at the entrance to Fort Renown, but they were seldom closed; even at night. The Choctaw, unlike some of their fiercer and more martial neighbours, could see which way the wind was blowing and knew that there was little enough point in fighting physically against the encroachment of white settlers on their lands. They made the best of things by driving hard bargains with the white folk for the raw materials they needed and, wherever possible, cheating them blind.

A sentry sat at the gate of the fort, whose job was to spot anybody entering the little town who might be after causing trouble. He nodded amiably to Saddler and Abigail, saying only,

'Welcome to Fort Renown. Specially welcome to you, young lady. It ain't often we get youngsters passing through here.'

'Tell me now,' said Saddler, 'is there anywhere I can leave these horses for the night?'

'Sure, there's a man runs a corral over there. It's outside the walls, but a boy watches the horses during the night. Nobody stolen one yet.'

Saddler and Abigail took their mounts over to the corral and removed the saddles and other gear. They left them in charge of the boy watching over the place, until they had somewhere to stay for the night.

The stockade of sharpened logs enclosed an area of just over eight acres. It had been made so large, because those who had built it had intended it to be a forward staging post for an entire army. It had never fulfilled its purpose and was for most of the war held only by a token force. A week after the surrender it had been abandoned.

The original buildings of the fort lined the walls and as newcomers arrived they threw up commercial premises built also of logs. Some of these were substantial: the saloon had three storeys, the top two of which were given over to a cathouse. It was a busy place, with white people bringing in produce from their farms, Indians selling ponies and hides, a few soldiers and many trappers and traders who spent a night or two in the place while they were moving across the territories. Saddler was pretty confident of finding somewhere for Abigail to be able to sleep soundly in a bed for the night.

'Why,' Abigail said in surprise, 'this is quite a civilized location.'

'You wouldn't say so, not if'n you knew what half these rogues was up to,' Saddler replied. 'Places like this attract all the gamblers, no-counts, vagabonds and plain villains as are within a hundred miles.'

'Can I go and look round by myself?' the girl asked brightly, not at all discouraged by Saddler's gloomy estimation of the types to found in Fort Renown. Saddler stopped dead and said,

'Listen to me right good, Abigail. This very morning you come within an ace of gettin' yourself killed. You flat disobeyed me when I told you to stay in the wagon during that little shooting we had. I want now that you listen to what I say. You are not to stray from my side for a second. Not one second, you hear what I tell you? This ain't a fit place for a little girl. No telling what would befall you. Some o' the boys as hang out here are a sight worse than any she-bear.'

'Perhaps later then,' said Abigail brightly.

Saddler shook his head in despair. He had discovered in recent days that tending to and keeping from harm a twelve-year-old girl child was the hardest enterprise he had undertaken since the end of the war. Breaking wild ponies and dealing with drunken killers was nothing compared with setting a watch upon a girl like Abigail. True, she made a better companion than many he had ridden with, but you never could gauge what was going on in the mind of such a one.

There was a respectable little hotel which was used by the better class of person who was travelling through the territories and it was to this that Saddler directed them. Calling the rough, wooden building a 'hotel' was perhaps flattering such a basic amenity, which in truth consisted of nothing more than six rooms, each containing an iron bedstead and little more. The owner of this enterprise lived in one of the rooms and had a minuscule sitting room at the front of the building, which doubled as an office. There were no eating facilities, the place was far too cramped for that, and anybody desirous of a bite to eat was obliged to try the saloon or buy their food from the store.

Saddler was all charm when he approached the owner of the hotel. The middle-aged woman eyed him with suspicion when he entered her office, but as soon as she caught sight of Abigail her mood changed. In her mind Saddler had been transformed from travel-stained vagabond into respectable family man.

'Say ma'am,' said Saddler, 'I was wondering if you had such a thing as a room for the night for this young lady?'

'Why surely we do. Will you be requiring a room for yourself too?'

'Do you have two spare rooms?'

'We have four tonight.'

'Well then, yes. That would be right nice of you if you could rent us two rooms.'

'Will that be just for tonight?'

Saddler thought for a moment and then said, 'Yes, for now. But I suppose if we wanted, we could always keep them for another night?'

The matter was attended to briskly and Saddler and Abigail were shown to two spartan, but clean and tidy, little rooms.

When he had paid the owner and she had left, Abigail said to Saddler, 'Are we going to look round the town now?'

It was so pleasant to observe the change in the child since first he had encountered her that Saddler did not like to repress her high spirits.

He said, 'Abigail, I will show you round here in a space, but first off is where we need to get things straight.'

'What things?' asked the child.

'You do not leave my side is one. Unless, that is, I tell you to. Is that plain?'

'That's fair, I guess. What else?'

'You do just as I say an' when I say. I say, 'We're leaving', you just stand up and come right with me. Without any chatter or aught of that kind.'

'I can do all that. I'm older than you mind. You treat me like I was six.'

'Six or twelve, it makes no odds. You're a child and I am answerable for you,' said Saddler. 'Mark now, 'less you agree, we are goin' nowhere in this town.'

'All right, Mr Saddler. I'll do just as you say.'

Having settled the case to his own satisfaction, although not without some inward misgivings as to the girl's ability to comply with such rules, Saddler suggested that they hunt out some food and then eat it out of doors.

'But first,' he said, 'You set here quietly, while I fetch in the saddles and so on.'

There were three stores in Fort Renown. One specialized in kitchen wares, domestic utensils, lamp oil and other such useful commodities as the local farmers and settlers would be needing. The second sold agricultural implements like hoes and spades, and also seed. It stocked food as well. The third dealt chiefly in clothes and firearms.

They bought a loaf of bread, a hunk of cheese, some cold meat and a pitcher of buttermilk and then left the fort to sit on the grass outside.

'This is nice,' said Abigail. 'It's like having a picnic. We used sometimes to have those, my parents and I. They were fun.'

Saddler listened with half an ear to the girl's chattering while keeping a sharp eye on those entering and leaving Fort Renown. Although it had been his own idea to come here he was a little uneasy in his mind and didn't quite know why.

'Did you hear what I said?' asked Abigail.

'No,' Saddler said frankly, 'I can't truthfully say as I did. Repeat it.'

'I said that I thought I saw that bad man who wanted to shoot you.'

'What? The hell you did! When?'

'While you were telling me to be good and follow your instructions. I was looking from the window and made sure that it was he, passing along the way. He had his arm in a sling.'

'Abigail, why the devil did you not tell me this earlier?'

She shrugged. 'Because I wouldn't take oath on it in a court of law. My pa told me that that should be your touchstone for repeating tittle-tattle and relating what you have seen. He used to say, 'If you wouldn't be prepared to take oath and swear to the thing in a court of law, then remain silent and do not pass on the gossip you hear'.'

'Lord, this ain't exactly gossip. It could mean life or death to us. I surely wish you'd mentioned this before.'

'I'm sorry. I hope I have not caused more trouble.'

'No, you're all right Abigail. Just speak out sooner next time, is all. If he's here, then I must hunt him out and settle matters.'

'You don't mean to shoot him?'

'No, but he might wish to kill me. If so, then I'd a heap sooner that I was facin' him, rather than having him go for my back. I want anything that fires up to be on my terms, not his.'

Abigail thought for a bit and then said, 'But we can still look around together, can't we?'

'Yes, but always recollecting what I told you. Which is to say, if I say 'stay there' or 'come here' or anything else, you do it at once.'

It was a beautiful sunny evening, and left to himself Ben Saddler would like as not have preferred to go for a stroll in the nearby woods. Howsoever, he could see that the child was just itching to look round Fort Renown and so, although he wasn't wholly easy about it, he agreed to take a turn round the place.

Saddler had been to many little towns a lot more interesting than this, but to Abigail the fort was evidently as exciting as a fairground. She stopped to look at everything, smiled at passers-by and kept up a stream of chatter. It struck Saddler that her parents must have kept a tight rein on the child, discouraging inconsequential conversation and forbidding play, as she had intimated to him. With those restraints lifted, she had been given the opportunity to behave like any other child of her age and it did him good to hear her talking so merrily.

'Can we visit the saloon?' asked Abigail.

'No, it's not to be thought of,' said Saddler, slightly appalled. 'I never heard o' such a thing. That ain't a place for a well-brought up girl like you to be seeing.'

'Oh, please. I never even looked in the window of a real saloon.'

It was this that caused Saddler to decide, against his better judgement, to let the girl at least look inside a saloon. In addition to being abolitionists and who knew what all else, he guessed that Abigail's parents had probably been temperance types as well; sworn to abstain from intoxicating liquor. It surely would do no harm for her at least to look in the door or through the window of The Girl of the Period. Saddler's reservations centered around the fact that the top two floors of that particular establishment were fitted out as a brothel, but he figured that if they just stood outside and looked in to the ground floor, where the drinking and gambling took place, it could not be likely to harm the child.

'Well,' said Saddler, 'I tell you what. We'll take a turn down that way and you can look through the windows and maybe see what's to be seen from the doorway. But we ain't going in no drinking hole, not while I got the care of you.'

Abigail smiled at him. 'Oh, thank you, Mr Saddler. My mother and father were very particular about drink, which they both said was the root of a lot of the evil in this world. I signed the pledge myself when I was just seven year of age.'

'Pledge?' said Saddler curiously.

'What pledge might that be?'

'Why,' said the child, scandalized at such ignorance, 'the pledge to abstain my whole life long from strong drink. There's scriptural backing for temperance, you know.'

Not for the first time since he had picked up with the child, Saddler uttered a silent malediction upon people who could bring up a lively little thing like this and hedge her in with so many harsh rules.

He said, 'I recall that nigh on the first thing Noah did after the flood was make some wine. Doesn't it say in the Bible that he was so liquored up that he fell over without his clothes on?'

'I didn't know that you read the Bible,' said Abigail. 'I got the feeling that you were a regular heathen.'

'So I am,' said Saddler. 'I was made to learn a heap of scripture in the orphanage. It never took though. Those as were the hottest for the word of the Lord were the biggest bastards in the place, if you'll pardon my language.'

By this time, they had reached the saloon and Saddler said to Abigail, 'Mind now, we ain't a goin' inside. I don't see no harm though in peeping in at the window.'

Abigail skipped up to the grimy window at the front of the building and looked through, into the dim and smoky interior.

'Can I look through the door?' she said.

'Yeah, you go right ahead.'

Abigail was not however fated ever to have a clear view of the inside of the saloon, because as she approached the batwing doors they were pulled back and a man strode out. His left arm was carried in a sling and he looked as mean as all-get-out. He recognized Abigail at once, because as soon as he caught sight of her he began looking round for her erstwhile companion. When he saw Saddler, he smiled crookedly and said,

'I got a crow to pluck with you, fellow.'

6

Ben Saddler did not make any sudden move, nor did he speak for a second or two. Then he said,

'You be Joe Collins, as was with my old partner Stock. Is that how it stands?'

'That it is. What become o' Stock?'

'I shot him down.'

'Is he dead?'

Saddler laughed out loud. 'You don't know me, do you Collins? When I shoot a man, I mean for to kill him dead. Abraham Stock died not two minutes after you dug up and ran.'

The other man flushed slightly on hearing Saddler claim that he had 'run'.

'You say what, you whore's son? You think I run away from you?'

'Watch your mouth. There's a child present.' Turning to Abigail, Saddler said, 'Abigail, you cut along now and set over there on the porch of yon' store.' He pointed to a building twenty-five yards or so from them. He was relieved when the girl at once trotted obediently off to sit where he had bid her. Once she was safely out of the way, he turned back to Collins.

'I got no quarrel with you,' he said. 'You an' Stock set up as bushwhackers and chose the wrong man to rob. That's how it goes sometimes. I ain't got a grudge.'

From Saddler's perspective the matter was quite simple and he was wholly in the right. Two men had tried to rob him and then come off worse. If he was happy to forget the business, then he was damned if he knew why the other party should be determined to carry on the dispute. It was over and finished and the man standing before him had escaped with his life. He ought to be counting his self lucky, not come now getting ready to cut up rough about the affair.

It was plain as a pikestaff that the

man called Joe Collins held a contrary view of the matter to that to which Saddler himself subscribed. Indeed, he said as much, reasoning out the case in this way:

'You shot my wrist. See here, where my arm is in a sling? Doctor says there's nothing to be done. The bone is smashed to atoms and I'm like to lose the hand. Even if I don't, it'll never be any use to me. You ever try riding with one hand?'

'I tried it once or twice,' admitted Saddler in a cheerful conversational tone. 'Tried it, but it didn't really answer. I always found it better to use both hands on the reins. Still and all, you can get used to 'most anything in time. Or so they say.'

'You made a cripple of me. Now you pay for it.'

'Truth is, Collins, I am mighty busy right now. That child over yonder, I am takin' her to her family. It's a long story, but I can't risk my life over this. I'm sorry about your hand, but you would a done better not to trouble me in the first place. Least you're still alive, which Abraham Stock is not. Leave it alone now and we'll go our own ways.'

'You think so? I'll have blood.'

The man's pigheadedness was beginning to irk Saddler and of a sudden, he lost patience, saying,

'All right you troublesome bastard, if you'll have it so. You'll have blood? Happen it'll be your own. I take it you're right-handed?'

'I am.'

'So you can draw well enough?'

'You'll see how well I can draw directly.'

Without taking his eyes off the fellow for the least fraction of a second, Saddler backed off, moving slowly into what passed for a street, the space separating the saloon from the nearby stores. Collins said nothing more but also moved slowly backwards, until the two of them were facing each other at a distance of some thirty feet. Passers-by hastened to move, so that they were not behind either of the men. From the resigned and practised way that they undertook this manoeuvre it was apparent that dodging stray bullets like this was not exactly a novelty for the residents of Fort Renown.

Collins was sporting a fancy rig of tooled black leather. He looked the part of a gunfighter far more than the shabby figure facing him in that street, with an old pistol tucked carelessly in his belt. Appearances are often deceptive, though, and in truth Saddler had not the least apprehension about the outcome of this contest. He was quicker than a rattlesnake at work of this sort and unless he mistook the man greatly, Joe Collins was already as good as dead.

The two of them stood there, neither venturing to draw. They held this position for something like a minute before Collins went for his pistol. He was quick enough, but had nowhere near Saddler's speed. The old Navy Colt was in his hand, cocked and levelled in the time that it took Collins to begin pulling his own pistol. Saddler fired twice, in quick succession. His first bullet took his opponent in the chest and before the man fell, he followed up with a more carefully aimed shot through the man's forehead. Joe Collins was dead before he hit the ground.

Saddler called out to the spectators, 'You all saw that. I gave him a fair chance. Anywise, I didn't even want this fight.'

It had been a clean contest and nobody would blame him for the death. He had started walking towards Abigail when a man from the watching crowd stepped forward. He was an older man, with a long, drooping white moustache. He had a silver star on his jacket and said,

'I'm a US marshal. You're under arrest.'

'What?' said Saddler in amazement. 'That was a fair fight an' he started it into the bargain. Ask any of those over by that there saloon.' He called out to a couple of loafers. 'You saw what happened. Tell the marshal here.'

The marshal gave a short, barking laugh. 'You think I give a shit if you trash kill each other? It's nothing to me. You don't call me to mind, do you, Saddler?'

Saddler looked closely at the man and then let out a resigned sigh. 'Aaah!'

'Yeah, that's right,' said the marshal. 'Aaah! You're Ben Saddler and there's a warrant outstanding against you.'

'A warrant? The hell are you talking about?'

'Six months ago you were running rifles into the territories. No,' he said, as Saddler began instinctively to deny the suggestion, 'you can save that for the judge. I'm taking you to Greensborough, where you'll stand trial.' Saying which, he reached out his hand and took Saddler's pistol from him. Then he took the unresisting man's arm and led him away from the scene of his late triumph against Joe Collins.

Abigail had watched the gunfight with great interest, never doubting for a single moment that Saddler would best the other. When the man came up afterwards and led Saddler away, she sensed that it would be better to keep her distance. As she trailed along a few paces behind them, she wondered if this was the same feeling that Mr Saddler had talked of, when he could just *feel* that trouble was brewing. Right now, she just *knew* that the best thing to do was hang back and see where her friend was being taken. From the way that Saddler allowed himself to be marched along like this and had meekly surrendered up his gun, Abigail guessed that this was a lawman.

Now Abigail Filer might only be twelve years of age and have led a pretty sheltered life into the bargain, but she was not a perfect fool. She had guessed soon after meeting him that Ben Saddler was a man who made his money in various ways that would not bear close examination. She also knew something else, and that was that beneath that devil-may-care exterior, beat a kind and loving heart. She was sure that Saddler was a fundamentally good man.

On a more practical level, he had promised to get her to her mother's folks in Kansas and she had the notion that he would not just make a few cursory enquiries to that end, but saw the matter more in the nature of being a holy duty. If some busybody found that she was wandering alone in the Indian Territories, then she was apt to be taken into charge and probably packed off to an orphans' asylum. Once there, the chances were that it would be very hard for anybody to make contact with her mother's folks, seeing as she didn't even know her mother's maiden name. She needed Mr Saddler and if that meant helping him to evade the law, then so be it.

As they walked along, Saddler said to the marshal, 'Were you looking for me here?'

Marshal Devlin snorted derisively, 'You think I got nothing better to do than go chasing after a saddle-bum like you? No, I had business hereabouts. It was just chance as set me in your path. I been after a pair of scamps, but they'll keep.'

'You couldn't let bygones be bygones, Devlin? I got pressing matters need attending to.'

'I'll be bound you have. What is it this time, Saddler? More guns for the Chickasaw? Moonshine for the Choctaw? No, you been dancing between the raindrops for long enough. Here is where you learn some respect for the law.'

'Not from you, I won't!' muttered Saddler.

Now as Marshal Devlin very well knew, his authority in the Choctaw nation was of a very tenuous and debatable nature. Had Saddler been prepared to make a fight of it, there would have been little enough that Devlin could have done to enforce his will. Still, he knew his man. People like Saddler might break the law and get up to all manner of mischief, but when faced by a man with a star, they would generally knuckle under, and so it had proved in the present circumstance.

Because there was no real law in Fort Renown, there was no jail or sheriff's office where a man like Ben Saddler could be held overnight. The town's vigilance committee, however, acknowledged the authority of any US marshal and went out of its way to cooperate and provide facilities for such men. Once before Devlin had needed somewhere to keep a man locked up overnight, and Jack Stoker, the head of the vigilance committee, had lent him the use of a storage shed out back of his premises. Stoker ran the agricultural provisions store.

Abigail tried to look inconspicuous as she stood outside the store next to Stoker's and watched as the marshal led Saddler in, then emerged a minute later with a large ring on which were a number of keys. He led his captive round the back of the store to a wooden shed. The child saw Saddler pushed roughly into this and the door locked behind him. Acting on an impulse, Abigail skipped quickly back into the store and began examining some zinc pails. The storekeeper ignored her. When Marshal Devlin returned with the keys she watched out of the corner of her eye as the man behind the counter hung them carelessly on a hook in the wall, just above his head.

Not wanting to draw attention to herself, Abigail left the store and tried to think out the best course of action. There would be no chance of sneaking into the store and simply taking that bunch of keys. No, she would need to get the storekeeper out of the way first. How if she brought him a message and told him that somebody in another part of the fort wished to see him? He might be fooled, but like as not he would then lock up his store behind him when he left. That wouldn't answer. What was needed was something which would get that man running out of his store without stopping to think about his keys or anything else. She would need to think about this real hard.

Sitting on the floor of the stinking, dark shed Saddler felt a wave of despair engulf him. It was not so much that he minded being carted back to Greensborough to have his role in a little gunrunning investigated. At worst he would be looking at a hefty fine or perhaps six months in the penitentiary. His chief concern was the child whom he had promised to help. What would become of a helpless orphan girl stuck alone in the middle of the Indian Territories? What would become of her now?

Sunk in such gloomy thoughts and beginning to wonder if he should not tell Devlin of the child's existence, so that some provision could be made for her, Saddler did not at first hear the soft scratching on the outside wall of his prison. Then a voice whispered,

'Are you all right in there, Mr Saddler?'

'Abigail? What are you about?'

'I'm going to get you out of there. Don't worry, I will have to go away for an hour or two, but be ready to leave when I unlock the door.'

'Unlock the door? What are you up to, child? Listen, you must find that marshal and tell him that you are alone here. He will make arrangements for you to be taken somewhere safe.'

'An orphanage, you mean? No, I will arrange things. I have to go now.'

'No, Come back, Abigail. What are you doing?' Saddler might as well have saved his breath. Abigail had evidently left, to undertake whatever plans she had formulated. He had been pleased to hear her voice, but had little hope that a child of such tender years would really be able to outfox that wily bastard Devlin.

Abigail went back to the rooming house, and after greeting the owner went into the room that Saddler had taken. Under the circumstances, she felt justified in going through his belongings, in order to see if there was anything that might help her to free him. Apart from his blanket and rifle there was little more than a flask of powder, a box of lucifers and a few other odds and ends. It did not seem to Abigail that she would be able to make much use of the rifle. She had never fired a gun in her life, and the time to begin was not on a desperate enterprise such as this. The powder, though; that might come in handy.

In all her twelve years Abigail Filer had never once cut loose and behaved in a riotous or even mischievous fashion. Perhaps it was holding back all those little devilments over the whole course of her childhood that contributed to the events that night. At any rate, she would soon make up for being so well behaved for over a decade. That same brain that had hitherto exercised itself with nothing more taxing than helping out in Sunday school was now devising a scheme so outrageous that even Ben Saddler himself might have been reluctant to embark upon it.

The saddles were heavy and Abigail knew that she would have to carry them out of Fort Renown one at a time. It would be necessary to tack up their mounts and then have them waiting near at hand because, if she followed the plan which was fermenting in her agile young mind, they needs must ride like the wind as soon as Saddler was free. On the landing outside the rooms was a can of lamp oil. That too would come in handy. This would be plain theft, but Abigail justified this sin to herself by recollecting that Saddler had paid for two rooms this night; neither of which would be occupied. Trading that off against a pint or so of lamp oil seemed to her a fair deal.

Getting the horses ready took considerably longer than Abigail had budgeted for. Each saddle was a journey to and from the place where they had booked the rooms. Then the blankets and so on were another two journeys. It was nearly nine before she had both horses tacked up and with their packs on them. The night in the corral had already, like their own rooms, been paid for. The boy watching over the animals asked if they were planning on leaving at once, but Abigail snubbed him and did not reply.

Now it was dark and, if she was going to undertake this business, it was time to do so. She felt breathless with anxiety. There was, at least as far as she knew, no scriptural justification for what she was about to do and she had little else upon which to draw. Certainly no real-life experience in her short life had given her any guidance on such a matter. Still, the only other choice was to go to that marshal and ask him to deliver her to the orphan's asylum in Greensborough at the same time as he deposited Mr Saddler in the jailhouse. I'm darned, she thought, no, I'm . . . damned if I'll do so.

There was no properly organized

collection of garbage in Fort Renown, so folk tended to chuck their rubbish out back of their premises, until it built up too high. Then they would agree an afternoon and cart it all out of the fort and start a bonfire. Some people had warned that all the old bits of broken wood, torn paper and rags which began to pile up against the wooden walls of the fort were a fire hazard. This was particularly so, because every single building in those eight acres was built of nothing other than wood.

It had been a dry, hot summer and clearing away all the current crop of litter was overdue. It was observing all the junk heaped up at back of the buildings that had given Abigail her idea; that and witnessing the destruction by fire of the Indian Bureau offices in the Chickasaw nation.

Without attracting too much attention to herself, Abigail made three little piles of smallish pieces of discarded wood, up against the logs which made up the wall of the stockade. She spaced

126

them thirty feet apart and made the first of them a little way along from the shed in which Saddler was confined. In the third of the piles, the one furthest from the shed, she carefully positioned the copper powder-flask that she had found among Saddler's things.

Then she gathered up bits of old newspaper, pieces of material and anything else flammable and pushed this kindling into the spaces between the pieces of wood which she had heaped up. There had been a church barbecue the previous summer at which she had helped out and she had been fascinated at how the fire had been started and maintained.

Over each of the three heaps she poured a little of the lamp oil that had been purloined from the rooming house.

It was quite dark by the time she had completed her preparations and Abigail crept to the shed behind the store.

'Mr Saddler,' she called softly, 'Are you awake?'

'I'm awake. Abigail, have you been to see Marshal Devlin and explained to him that you are alone and helpless?'

'Not quite.'

'Not quite? What the . . . deuce does that mean?'

'In a minute I'll have the key to this place. I've saddled up the horses and they're ready to go. We will have to ride in the dark, but I dare say you know how to do that.'

'What are you talking about, child? You can't spring me from here. You mustn't think of such a thing, it would make you a felon.'

'Be ready in a few minutes. I'll be back with the key.'

Saddler felt a cold hand clutch at his heart.

'Abigail, you stop this nonsense right now, you hear what I say?' There was no answer. He called slightly louder, 'Abigail!' It was obvious that the child had gone.

Saddler was worried out of his mind. What on earth could she be about? He was terrified that she would get into trouble herself. He would never forgive himself if he was responsible for a child that age getting into hot water with the law.

After leaving Mr Saddler and pretending that she couldn't hear his frantic shouts for her to stop, Abigail went round to the front of the store again. Like most of the businesses in Fort Renown, the stores did not generally open until late morning and then carried on trading until after dark, or until there were no more customers. Through the window she could see the owner or clerk or whatever he was, sitting behind the counter and studying some ledgers. In the yellow gleam of the oil lamp, she could just make out the big ring of keys hanging on the wall near to him.

Clutching the box of lucifers tightly in her hand, Abigail returned to the back of the store and made her way cautiously along the wall of the fort towards the furthest of the piles she had built up. The air reeked with the smell of the kerosene which she had poured over it. Before she could give herself the chance to change her mind, Abigail struck one of the long matches and dropped it on to the oil soaked heap of junk. There was a whoosh and yellow flames leapt up into the night air.

7

Dripping as the pile of trash was with lamp oil, the flames took a fierce hold much faster than Abigail would have thought. She moved swiftly to the next collection of rubbish and set that alight as well. Then, without stopping, she ran to the final heap, the one nearest to the shed in which Saddler was imprisoned and threw a lighted match on that.

Her heart pounding with a heady mixture of fear and excitement, Abigail ran round to the front of the store and rushed through the door. The owner looked up in surprise at such a precipitate entrance.

'Whoa, there,' he said, 'Where's the fire?'

'That's just it,' said the girl breathlessly. 'There is a fire. Just round the back of your store.'

'If this is a game, young lady,' began

the man and then stopped in amazement. There was a loud explosion, as
the flask of powder which Abigail had
placed at the heart of one of the fires
went off.

'Oh, do hurry,' she said, 'I think it
must be spreading.'

The man pulled off the blue-and-
white striped apron that he wore when
working in the store and then hesitated
for a moment.

Abigail said, 'Don't stop to lock up
and put out the lamp. I'll wait here and
mind the store for you.'

Jack Stoker nodded and then, without another word, ran outside. It was
the work of a moment for the child to
reach up and grab the bunch of keys,
then dart back out again and open up
the shed where Saddler was being held.

'Quick!' she cried, 'We have to leave
now.'

Saddler came out of the shed and
glanced to his left. The scene that met
his eyes was an apocalyptic one. The
three fires that Abigail had started were

blazing away merrily, but that was not all. The explosion of the powder flask had flung burning material and sparks on to the garbage that was scattered all along the space between the back of the buildings and the wooden wall of the stockade. As a consequence, flames were now licking up the backs of the stores, as well as threatening to burn down the walls of the fort.

'God almighty, Abigail,' exclaimed Saddler in horror, 'what've you done?'

'I had to make a distraction, so that I could get the keys,' replied the child impatiently. 'But it will all be for nothing if we don't get out of here now.'

'Where's the horses?'

'In the corral. I tacked them up.'

'Good girl,' said Saddler, in reluctant admiration at the child's resourcefulness. 'I guess you're right, we have to go right now.'

Nobody bothered to cast a glance at the two figures who slipped through the shadows and out of the main gate to Fort Renown. The case was too desperate for the citizens of the town to do other than focus their whole efforts upon preventing their homes and livelihoods from being consumed by the flames. Every available receptacle was pressed into service in the attempts to save the town; the contents of buckets, bottles, pitcher and even chamberpots were flung on the fires in a desperate bid to extinguish them. One intoxicated fool even poured a bottle of brandy on to some smouldering rags and was rewarded by seeing them flare instantly into blue flames.

The horses in the corral were jittery, and if the fire got any worse Saddler could see them all getting seriously spooked. The watchman was nowhere in sight and so Saddler vaulted over the fence and led Abigail's pony to the side. He secured his reins to a post and then went back for his own mount. Then he led both horses to the gate and threw it open. The other animals took the chance to bolt for freedom. With any luck, Marshal

Devlin's horse would be among them.

When the two of them had mounted, Abigail said, 'Which way are we going?'

'Up there, towards the woods. I want to get off the open country soon as can be.'

A gentle rise led to the woods. When Fort Renown had been built this area had been all over wooded, and the stumps of the trees that had once grown here were scattered thickly around.

Saddler said, 'Mind where you're guiding that beast. Keep to the track, I don't want either of these horse being lamed.'

When they reached the edge of the wood Saddler pulled up and turned to look back at the town. It looked to him as though the fire was under control, but it must have been a close-run thing. The more distance he and Abigail put between themselves and the inhabitants of Fort Renown the better. Little actions like this were the kind of thing that set lynching parties into action. He shook his head in disbelief and turned to the girl at his side.

'What in the hell was you thinking of, Abigail? You might o'killed folks back there.'

'Aren't you glad to be free?'

He was thankful that the darkness hid the smile that came unbidden to his lips. He contented himself with saying, 'The sooner we get you living with respectable folks again, the better. Strikes me as associatin' with me ain't exactly improved your character none.'

It was dark in the forest and they proceeded at a walk. After they had been travelling for a little while, Abigail said, 'Do you think that they will be able to track us?'

'You mean figure out which way we went? No, I wouldn't've said so. There's so much coming and going into that town, they won't be able to identify our hoof-marks. Still and all, the further we get before dawn the better I'll like it.'

'Are you cross with me for setting those fires? It was all I could think of.'

'I ain't cross with you, Abigail,' said Saddler. 'You're a child. You did the best you could, given the circumstances. It comes of riding with a scamp like me.'

'What would you have done, had you been in my place?'

Saddler didn't answer for a spell and then he said, 'Truly? I would o' most likely done the same as you did. But that don't make it right.'

Having been reassured that the man at her side wasn't angry, Abigail began rather to enjoy the journey through the woods. It was dark and mysterious, but she knew that as long as Saddler was at her side, he would protect her from any danger.

Although he was, not unnaturally, pleased to be free of the shed in which that bastard Devlin had confined him, Ben Saddler was feeling a twinge of guilt that after only a few days in his company a little girl should think it a good scheme to try and burn down a town. He could attribute it only to his bad influence and he genuinely felt that he had corrupted the child. She surely would not have come up with such a wild notion, had she still been in the care of decent, God-fearing people. The sooner he could get her back to civilization the easier he would be in his mind. The last thing he wished was to be the cause of her turning out wrong.

It was a funny thing, but since hitching up with that child, Saddler's conscience had been getting more exercise than it had done for the preceding decade. He hadn't ever put it into words, but if he had, Ben Saddler would perhaps have described his conscience as an essentially vestigial organ, a bit like his appendix. He knew it was there and supposed that it had once served some useful purpose, but he seemed able to progress quite happily through life without making any use of it.

The pair rode on for maybe three hours. Saddler realized that they would need to stop when he saw Abigail's pony wandering off to one side.

He called out, 'Hey, get that horse back on the path, child.'

There was no answer and so he spoke more sharply. It was at that point that he knew that the little girl had simply fallen asleep. He rode over and halted the pony. Then he dismounted and shook Abigail gently, saying,

'You're asleep, sweetheart.'

'Oh, I'm sorry,' she said, lifting her head up in surprise. 'I was having such a lovely dream. My parents were . . . were . . . still here.'

'Let's get off the road aways and we'll rest up for the night.'

Saddler led the two horses into the woods for a quarter-hour. Then, when they came to a grassy stretch, he halted and lifted Abigail down from the pony.

After he had tucked the sleepy child up in her blanket and settled his own self down for the night, Saddler lay in the dark, listening. His ears were straining in particular for any sounds such as might be made by a party of angry riders, looking for a fire-raiser whom they could string up from the nearest tree. There was nothing, other than the normal forest murmurs.

Before pulling his own blanket round him for the night, he had, by the light of a lucifer, sorted through the packs. There was enough for breakfast and possibly a light meal later in the day, but that was all. He had hoped to buy a heap of provisions at Fort Renown, but that wasn't how it had turned out at all. Well, he thought, that's how it is sometimes. You make a lot of plans and then things conspire to set those same plans at naught.

Question was, what was to be done the next day? Didn't scripture say something about, 'Sufficient unto the day is the evil thereof'? Meaning, he supposed, that there wasn't a deal of use fretting about what you would be doing tomorrow. So thinking, he drifted into the arms of Morpheus.

Saddler was catapulted into con-sciousness the next morning by the sharp, metallic and unmistakable click of a pistol being cocked by his ear. He did not move a muscle, knowing that in such a position sudden movements can prove fatal. Instead, he turned his eyes slowly to the direction from which the sound had come and then threw off the blanket and jumped wrathfully to his feet.

'Jackson, you cowson,' he said angrily. 'What the hell are you playin' at?'

The man squatting on the ground shrugged equably. 'Had a wager with my brother,' he said, quite unabashed. 'Told him you was so fast asleep, I could get the drop on you. I guess I win.'

From behind a tree stepped another young man, almost the spit-image the fellow who had shoved his gun in Saddler's ear. The Jackson brothers were separated in age by a little over a year. They could have been twins though, so similar were they in outward appearance. Both had lustrous, black curls and each had merry, dancing blue eyes. Tyler, the boy who had jumped Saddler, was twenty and his brother Jake was twenty-one.

Now a lot of the white men who roamed round the Indian territories trying to scrape a living were mean characters, such as you might not care to spend too much time with. Others were like Saddler; men who were basically sound, but who would do some pretty tough things when the need arose or if they were being pushed into a corner. The Jackson brothers, though, were in a class of their own. They were the most cheerful and good-natured young fellows you could hope to meet: always smiling, never out of sorts and the most engaging company you could wish for. Only problem was, neither of the boys was completely right in the head. They weren't what you might call crazy, there was something worse than that wrong with the brothers.

Most bad men know very well that they are doing wrong. Even while they are stealing, cheating and killing they know that they shouldn't be carrying on so. Tyler and Jake Jackson simply didn't have any idea about such things. They took what they wanted, did just as they pleased and the devil take the hindmost. They were great ones for acting on impulse and then dealing later with any unpleasant consequences. The very words 'right' and 'wrong' meant nothing to them. Saddler had known them for a couple of years and always found them agreeable fellows to spend an evening with, but had taken good care not to get mixed up with any of their adventures.

'What brings you two scallywags to this neck of the woods?' Saddler asked, 'Got some robbery in mind?'

Both the brothers laughed. Then they noticed Abigail, who was just waking up. 'Who's your little friend, Saddler?' asked Jake.

'I'm taking care of her for a space,' he

replied. 'It's by way of being a long story.'

'Hidy, miss,' said Tyler, winking at Abigail. 'How'd you fetch up with this fellow?'

'Never mind about that,' said Saddler hastily. 'Which way are you boys headed?'

'Truth is, Saddler,' said Tyler, 'we's on the lam.'

'What you done now?'

'Ah nothing to speak of, we had us a run-in with a real pile o' piss. Fellow called Devlin.'

Saddler's heart sank and he said, 'Thaddeus Devlin would that be? US marshal?'

'Hey, that's right. You know him?'

'You might say so. How's it you two fell foul o' him?'

'You got anything to eat, Saddler?' asked Tyler Jackson. 'Me and my brother here are purely starving to death. We can all sit down an' we'll tell you the story.'

'We're not overburdened with provisions, but I guess we can share what we do have,' Saddler said.

The three men and the child settled themselves comfortably on the mossy floor of the forest and Tyler Jackson explained how it was that Marshal Devlin was determined to catch him and his brother and see them banged up in the penitentiary.

'It happened in this wise, Saddler, and you, little missy. Me and Jake were out and about, stopping folk at odd times and helping 'em on their way by relieving them of any heavy burdens as they might be unable to bear.'

'He means robbing travellers,' Saddler explained to Abigail in an aside, the girl looking puzzled at Tyler Jackson's roundabout way of explaining his activities.

'Anywise, the two of us was behind some trees and saw a man coming. He looked a pleasant fellow, not too young and aggressive. Big white moustache; why he looked like your favourite uncle. I popped out from the front and Jake came from behind and he knew at once that there was no point going for his gun. Jake had a sawn-off twelve-gauge aimed at his back, like to have cut him in half had he made any unfriendly move.

'Well, it wasn't 'til then that I noticed he was sporting a star, but it was a mite late to stop. He cussed us up hill and down dale, I can't repeat the language he used, not in the presence of this young lady, but he spoke something' awful. Threatening us with jail and I don't know what all else.'

Jake interrupted his brother at this point, saying, 'Had he not been so damned rude, we might o' let him alone. After taking his money, that is.'

'So you took his money,' said Saddler. 'What else?'

'Well,' said Tyler, 'Jake here was mad at the things that Devlin was saying to us. He was calling us all the bastards under the sun. Oh, excuse me, little lady, it just slipped out.'

'That's quite all right,' said Abigail politely. 'I am used to strong language.

Mr Saddler here uses a deal of it himself.'

The brothers guffawed with laughter at that, in which Abigail joined; although she couldn't really see the joke. This was part of the Jackson brothers' charm: they created a pleasant and relaxed atmosphere.

'Where was I?' said Tyler Jackson. 'Oh yeah, Jake getting mad. He desired the old gentleman to get off his horse and then told him to strip buck naked. Pardon the expression, Miss Abigail. Well, Devlin, we had the draw on him and he was forced to comply. Then we set his horse running and told the fellow to walk off aways. We took his guns and everything else that was worth having among his belongings.'

'Which is how we found out his name and profession,' interjected Jake. 'He had a card-case and some official documents to identify him as a US marshal.'

'Who's telling this tale, you or me?' asked his brother irritably. 'Well now,

Jake here was still vexed with this here Devlin and so he did something quite disgusting.'

'What did he do?' asked Abigail.

'I hardly like to say in front of a nicely brought-up young lady like yourself,' said Tyler. 'Fact is, Jake pi . . . that is to say he made water all over the marshal's clothes, where they were lying there on the ground.'

Saddler made an exasperated noise. 'Ah, you pair of idiots. No wonder he's intent on tracking you down. That Devlin's a man never forgets a grudge. I can tell you now, he's back there a little way, in Fort Renown.'

'He's that close? Lord, we was thinking of popping down there for some vittles. Thanks for the tip, Saddler.'

Saddler had no particular desire to prolong his meeting with the Jackson brothers. He was not keen on Abigail spending time in their company. After her actions the previous night at Fort Renown, he felt guilty about having corrupted the child. He was pretty sure that the child would not have set out to nearly burn down an entire town had she still been with her parents or other respectable people. It must have been the effect of spending time with him that had caused her to behave in such a lawless fashion and he was worried about it. What she would end up like if she listened too long to the Jackson brothers, he shuddered to think. *Lord, she'll be taking up as a road agent before her thirteenth birthday at this rate!*

Abigail had taken to Tyler and Jake, both of whom treated her with great courtesy. Although utterly lacking in conscience themselves, they sometimes recognized innocence and virtue in others, and seemed to Saddler to be treating the child with the proper degree of respect. While Jake was telling Abigail some ridiculous anecdote, which was making her smile and sometimes laugh out loud, Tyler said that he would like a few words alone with Saddler. The two of them stepped a distance, although not so far that Saddler could not keep an eye on Abigail.

'Saddler, are you and that child wanting to get out of the territories?'

'Yes. That's so.'

'Which way you heading?'

'North. Why'd you ask?'

''Cause that's where we heading too. Kansas.'

Saddler shook his head. 'No, life with you boys is apt to be a little too lively for me, Tyler. I reckon me and the girl will travel by our own selves.'

'There's safety in numbers. You know the Chickasaw have risen?'

'Yeah, but we ain't aiming to go that way. We goin' north east.' Saddler did not feel it necessary to share his first-hand knowledge of events in the Chickasaw nation with the Jacksons.

'I'll lay down my cards, Saddler, and then see what you say. We need another couple o' horses . . . '

Tyler had hardly got the words out of

his mouth, before Ben Saddler turned a cold eye upon him.

'Don't you try to put the bite on me, Jackson. Last person as tried that game died real soon. Remember Abraham Stock?'

'Hey, I remember old Stock. How's he doing these days?'

'He's not. I killed him a couple o' days back. For doing much what you are fixin' to do. Don't do it, Jackson. The game's not worth the candle.'

Tyler Jackson laughed. 'You are one hasty man. Just let me set out my wares and then see what you say. All the white men like me and you who pass through the Indian nations are marked by the Indians. When a devil like that Devlin is chasing you, he offers rewards and so on, and the Indians often point out your tracks. Sometimes, they kill people and claim rewards. You know all that.'

This was all perfectly true and Saddler had already been calculating how he and Abigail would be able to move from this area without Thaddeus

Devlin catching their scent. He said to Jackson, 'Go on.'

'Well, me and my brother found a way round that difficulty, a way to move right through the territories without anybody passing word back to that bastard Devlin.'

Saddler was all ears now. He wasn't yet about to throw in with the Jacksons, but he surely was keen to hear of any scheme to escape Devlin's notice.

Tyler Jackson was watching him narrowly and observed, 'You goin' to be as open with us as I am bein' with you? Just what're you and that little girl up to, hidin' out in these here woods?'

'All in good time. Tell us what you purpose and then we'll see what's to do.'

'Are you on the run from Devlin as well?' asked Tyler Jackson shrewdly. 'Lord God, I can see it in your eyes. You are, aren't you? Well I'm damned.'

Saddler made a sudden decision. 'Listen, why don't we all sit down over yonder with your brother and see what

we are about. We needs must be open
and honest, but I tell you now, my main
concern is for the safety of that child.'

8

Saddler tried to persuade Abigail to go off and collect wild flowers or find some other distraction, while he and the Jackson brothers made medicine, but she wouldn't hear of it. She was polite and subdued, but obstinate as a mule.

'This is my affair, just as much as it is yours, Mr Saddler,' she said quietly. 'Why, if not for me, we might not be sitting here now.'

'How's that?' said Jake Jackson, 'What's the story there?'

Saddler gave him a very brief account of the previous night's adventures. Both the Jacksons smiled broadly to hear of Marshal Devlin's efforts being set at naught and, to Saddler's disgust, Tyler turned to Abigail, saying, 'Smart work, little miss.'

'It weren't smart work, at all,' Saddler said. 'It was a terrible thing to do and

I'll thank the two of you not to encourage such recklessness. Now you have our reasons for wantin' to avoid Devlin and you told us yours. How do you say we can travel to Kansas and not be the object of remark by Indians and others? And why'd you need our horses?'

'Like as not, you know that Wells Fargo are in trouble? Can't compete with all the new railroads.'

'I heard,' said Saddler.

'Well, most o' them routes they got running east to west, they're giving up. They starting to run to and from places the railroads don't cover. Chiefly, those going from north to south.'

'Tyler, if you want to give geography lessons, then you might get a school-house to engage you for the job. Get to the point,' said Saddler.

'Just a month ago Wells Fargo started running coaches from Texas to Kansas. They take through the Choctaw and Seminole nations and avoid Arkansas. Means no road tolls and cutting some hundreds of miles off the journey. They using some nice Concorde coaches. Beautiful things, with painted pictures on the doors and I don't know what all else.'

'Well,' said Saddler patiently, 'where does this tie in with us?'

'Me and Jake here, we got one o' their stages. Got it tucked away in a cave, not three miles from this very spot.'

'What?' cried Saddler. 'You mad fools have stolen a stagecoach?'

Neither of the brothers appeared to find anything odd about the situation. They didn't go into overmuch detail, but, from all that Saddler could collect, they had held up the stage and then for some reason taken into their heads, after having robbed the passengers, to hang on to the vehicle in which those passengers had been travelling. They had left the driver and his mate stranded in the middle of the Choctaw nation, along with those who had been travelling in the stage. Then they had driven it to one of their hideouts, backed it into the cave and covered the entrance with a load of brushwood.

After hearing this story, Saddler exclaimed, 'That is the damnedest thing I ever heard. You boys are something else again.'

'So,' said Tyler Jackson, 'here's how I read it. Devlin will have put out the word that he is looking for two young men with fresh faces and black, curly hair. Handsome fellows, as might turn a young lady's eye.' He winked at Abigail, who giggled.

He continued, 'From what you say, he will also be sending out for anybody to tell him of a man travelling alone with a little girl. Which is not what I would call a common sight in this part of the world.'

'You're thinking,' said Saddler thoughtfully, 'If we were in a stage, then Abigail here could ride inside and you boys could take it in turns to be up on the driving seat. Nobody would be thinking twice to see a Wells Fargo coach passing through?'

'You got it,' said Jake. 'What d'you say?'

Abigail broke in at this point, saying, 'Oh please let's, Mr Saddler. I'm getting awful tired of riding.'

'It might work,' said Saddler slowly. 'It just might. You two told me everything? No nasty surprises waiting?'

The whole idea sounded to Saddler as though it had much to recommend it. Abigail was still not a very fast rider and he had been wondering how long it would take them to get through to Kansas at the speed at which they had been travelling so far. And, as the Jacksons had pointed out, there was now the added complication of having that bastard of a marshal on their tail.

After the fire last night, and his escape, Saddler couldn't imagine for a moment that Thaddeus Devlin would simply mark the matter down to experience and forget all about him. He would speak to people today who would have remembered him and Abigail together, and he didn't need the Jacksons to tell him that a white man and a little girl made a rare and noticeable combination in the Choctaw nation.

'All right,' said Saddler, after turning it over in his mind for a spell, 'I'll buy it. I suppose that you need four horses for this coach? What became of those as was already harnessed up to it?'

'Sold 'em, of course,' said Tyler promptly. 'What d'you think we done with 'em?'

'Lord knows, with you two. Listen, the pair of you come over here with me. Abigail, you stay there a second.'

When he had led the brothers out of earshot of the curious child, Saddler said, 'One thing I'd have you two recall and that is that the girl is no more than a child. I don't want a heap of cursing and strong language or lewdness nor nothing else tending that way. Is that understood?'

Both the Jacksons laughed at this, Jake remarking to his brother, 'Shit, he

159

thinks we don't know how to behave like decent folk.'

'I mean it,' said Saddler and the two of them nodded.

Both Saddler and the two brothers were pretty eager to be making tracks from that part of the territories. All three of them had it at the back of their minds that at any moment Thaddeus Devlin would pop out from behind a tree and take them into custody. He might be getting on a little in years, but Marshal Devlin was a regular Tartar with wrongdoers, especially those who had wronged him personally.

Anxious about delays, Saddler asked if either of the brothers had the correct time and was surprised when Tyler pulled out an enormous gold hunter.

'Nice watch,' Saddler said. 'You inherit it or what?'

'Why, the fact is that this here belonged to that Devlin.'

'You even took his watch? No wonder he is vexed with you.'

Jake cut in at this point, saying, 'Had

he not been so damned rude, we would o'just took his money.'

'Let me see that watch,' said Saddler. 'It looks like something a man would set store by.'

The watch was so heavy that Saddler could tell at once that it wasn't pinchbeck. He opened the back and saw an inscription. Peering closely, he read, *To my dear son Thaddeus, from his proud father 4.7.41.*

'You fool,' Saddler said. 'You read this here?'

'No,' Tyler said. 'Me and my brother aren't great shakes at reading and ciphering and suchlike. What's it say?'

'His father gave him this watch when he was about twenty or something. No wonder he's mad as hell at the two of you. What ails you boys, that you always have to go that bit too far?'

It took less than a half hour to get to the cave off the road where the Jacksons had stowed the stolen stage-coach. It was a real beauty, with bright red coachwork. The doors, as the Jacksons had said, each bore an attractive painting of some pastoral scene. Prominently displayed above each door was the name of Wells Fargo.

'It's lovely,' cried Abigail as soon as she set eyes on it. 'So fresh and new. I never rode in a stage before. Oh, this is going to be such an adventure.'

Tyler and Jake Jackson were pleased at the child's reaction and began pointing out to Abigail various features of the stage that she might have overlooked, when Saddler cut in and reminded them that time was pressing.

'We don't any of us want Marshal Devlin riding down on us at the head of a posse, I wouldn't o' thought? Happen we can talk once we're on our way.'

It took the full strength of all three men to push the vehicle out of the cave and get it nigh to the road. Hitching up the horses was the devil of a job; not least because Abigail's pony did not fit well in harness with the other three full-size horses belonging to the men.

'Can I ride up there with the driver?'

asked Abigail, excited at the whole notion of a trip in a stagecoach.

'Abigail,' Saddler told her seriously, 'you are the most noticeable member of the whole, entire party. It is bad enough having Tweedledum and Tweedledee here, but we can split them up so that only one at a time can be seen. You would be spotted at once.'

'She's wearing pants,' Tyler said. 'Maybe if she tucks her hair out of the way, people won't have her pegged for a girl.'

'I'll thank you to tend to your own affairs,' Saddler told him sharply. 'This child's welfare is my business.'

After much debate it was agreed that having both Jackson brothers in view at the same time would be undesirable. Devlin might very well be asking if anybody had seen two similar-looking young men with those distinctive blue eyes and black, curly hair. They were to take it in turns to ride in the coach, while one was up in the driver's seat with Saddler. Abigail was to remain in the coach at all times. The girl was mightily displeased at this, but Saddler was immovable, and with an exceedingly bad grace Abigail agreed.

Before they set off Saddler asked the brothers, 'Have either of you any idea how often the genuine stages travel along this here road?'

Tyler and Jake shrugged; they neither of them had given the question any thought.

Saddler continued: 'What are we to do if we encounter a real Wells Fargo coach? Do we just ignore them, or what?'

This too had not occurred to the boys.

'Strikes me,' said Saddler, 'as you two haven't thought this thing through too closely.'

Fortunately for all concerned Saddler had some slight experience of driving a stage. He wasn't real good at it, but at least he knew the basics. Tyler and Jake were both raring to have a turn, but Saddler was more interested in getting as far from Fort Renown as was possible and so suggested that it would be wise if, that day, he alone took the reins.

Actually, Saddler enjoyed driving the stage. It demanded a good deal of work, ensuring that the four horses did as they were directed, but it made a change from riding. The Jackson brothers were both amiable fellows and he found it amusing to listen to their wild stories about the exploits in which they had recently been engaged. If you took the two of them on their own terms and did not expect too much in the way of normal, human morality, then Tyler and Jake were agreeable enough company. Saddler didn't trust either of them, but as things were going, it seemed to him that he and the child were better off travelling in this way.

The trouble at Fort Renown, being arrested and so on, had frightened him. Not because of what might have become of him, but on account of that little girl damn near got stuck alone in the Indian territories, with nobody to care for her. For all their shortcomings and mad ways, Saddler had a suspicion that if some harm befell him, the Jacksons might take care of Abigail and see that she was taken to safety. For that reason alone, it had been a smart move to team up with them.

The morning wore away pleasantly and they were making good time. The road along which they went was a little wider than most of the tracks through the territories, and presumably Wells Fargo felt that it was good enough for their coaches. It was a bumpy ride inside, from what his passengers reported, but that was only to be expected. Saddler was beginning to be pretty optimistic about his prospects of reaching Kansas with the child within another three days; four at the outside.

'What we goin' to do for food?' asked Tyler, who was sitting next to him.

'I don't know. I guess we'll have to

buy some or maybe shoot us some game.'

'Buy?' said Tyler in amazement. 'What for? We can just hit some place when we come by it. Take what we need.'

'Are you and that brother of yours completely loco?' asked Saddler, in a sympathetic tone, like he might have been enquiring after somebody's cold or fever. 'You think we can roll up in a Wells Fargo stage, rob somebody and then just leave and nobody will later remember us or remark to others on what a singular occurrence has befallen them that day? How many robbers ride round these parts in their very own Concorde coach? For God's sake, think what you're about, Jackson.'

'Me and Jake ain't got a mort o' cash money to buy goods with. Stealin's easier.'

'I have enough to get us some vittles. I reckon I owe you and Jake for this, anywise. It will be my payment for the journey.'

'Why, that's right nice of you, Saddler,' said Tyler. 'We'll just have to keep our eyes skinned for some farm or drinking den or whatever.'

As they travelled, Saddler could everywhere see the evidence of white men encroaching upon what was supposed in theory to be Indian land for all time. There were odd homesteads, surrounded by little patchworks of cultivated fields and then, here and there, larger stretches of farmed countryside. Little by little, the 'Indian' territories were being transformed into just another bit of the frontier; gradually being turned into a civilized, white district. Saddler thought to himself that if he was one of the Indians living here, then he too might be getting a little ticked off to see his land being stolen in this flagrant way and nobody from the government caring to do a damned thing about it.

By the time they came across the trading post, all four of them were feeling pretty hungry. In appearance, the place was just like Abbot's; a large, stone built house with a store at the front and little bar at the back. They pulled up outside and Saddler jumped down. Jake and Abigail opened the doors and climbed down. Oddly, nobody was about and there seemed to be no sign of life.

Saddler said, 'Abigail, you stay here with these boys. I'm going to look inside.'

There was nobody in the store and Saddler's shouts brought nobody out. He went round the back and found the owner. He was a stout man in early middle age. To Saddler's practised eye it looked like he had died hard. The man was spread-eagled against the back door of his home, fixed in place by three bayonets and so covered in arrows that he looked like a damned porcupine. There was nothing about the arrows to indicate which tribe had killed him.

'Tyler, you come with me. Jake, take a care of Abigail there, please.'

Saddler led Tyler Jackson round the back of the building and showed him what he had found. It was not the sort of thing as was likely to evoke any normal, human feelings in either of the Jacksons, and all that Tyler said was, 'I guess this means we won't have to pay for what we take?'

Saddler had an abhorrence at the idea of looting the dead, founded in his army days, where stealing from a dead man was viewed as the lowest kind of crime. Still and all, their need was desperate and so he and Tyler loaded up the stage with as many provisions as they were able. All the time Saddler was scanning the horizon, expecting a war party to heave into view at any second.

The murder of the man out the back had confirmed what he had been suspecting for a while now, which was that the murder of Abigail's parents, the destruction of the Indian Bureau and various other little incidents were not disconnected and random events. The territories were boiling over with indignation at the behaviour of the white men, and what was now happening was, as near as damn it, a general uprising involving at least three and probably four tribes.

Abigail didn't ask what had been found at back of the trading post and Saddler supposed that this was because she had already guessed. They decided to drive on and then stop a way down the road to eat.

They drove on for a half-hour and then halted near a little stream. They had brought a sack of feed for the horses and Saddler saw to them before they themselves ate. Saddler and Abigail were sober and thoughtful during the meal, both thinking of the circumstances in which they had met. The Jackson brothers, though, either did not fully apprehend the danger or, more likely, did not care about it. It would take more than the sight of a crucified man to dampen their zest for life.

Tyler said, after they had been eating

for a while, 'You want we should carry on the same trail, Saddler?'

'I don't see as we've another choice. This here will get us out o' the territories soonest.'

'You want we should prepare for trouble?'

Saddler did not really want to talk this over in front of the child, but Abigail didn't show any signs of being distressed, so he said,

'I don't have a pistol. That Devlin took it from me. I got my rifle up with me. Happen it'd be a wise move if whichever o' you boys was riding inside were to have his own rifle ready. Other than that, I don't see there's much to be done.'

'You got powder and shot for your gun?'

'Got no powder,' said Saddler.

'You want some?' asked Jake.

'Sure. Thanks.'

It came as no surprise to any of the three men, and probably not the child either, when shortly after starting out again they found themselves the object of unfavourable attention from a group of a dozen riders. Saddler was concentrating on controlling the horses and in particular balancing Abigail's pony against the three larger beasts, and so it was Jake Jackson, sitting next to him, who first saw the warriors riding along parallel to them.

'We got company,' Jake said, 'Over yonder to your right.'

'Ah, shit. I just knew that this was goin' to happen.' Saddler reached back and rapped sharply on the roof of the coach, causing Tyler to stick his head out of the window and ask what the problem was.

'Over to the right, there,' said Saddler.

'Them boys?' asked Tyler. 'Why, I seed them long time back. I'm a-ready when they are. What about you and my brother up there? You want to stop and parley?'

'The hell I do!' exclaimed Saddler. 'We'll have to make a run for it.'

He wished that he could have been in the coach, ready to reassure and comfort Abigail, and for a moment, Saddler thought about changing places with Jake and letting him take the reins. But both the Jackson boys were mad as coots and prone to taking the craziest chances. Jake would overturn the coach for sure and then they would all be done for.

Saddler reached down and brought his rifle up on to his lap. He cocked it and then whipped on the horses, wondering if they would be able to outride the men moving in on them. From the look of it, he gauged that they would be intercepting the stage in another five or ten minutes.

In the normal way of things, Saddler was a great one for waiting until others had made the first aggressive move, before responding. That way, there could be no doubt that he was acting in self-defence, which, if nothing else, was a sop for his conscience. He also had a deep-rooted horror of behaving like an assassin and striking when the other party was unawares. In the present case, though, none of these considerations seemed to him to apply. So he said to Jake, 'What say? We wait 'til they get closer or fire on them now and hope to scare 'em off?'

Jake's experience in such matters was extensive and he had no nerves at all to speak of.

'We don't fire yet,' he said, 'not by my reckoning. You'd not hit 'em at this range and it would be a waste of powder. 'Less you're hoping to scare them away? You think those boys are playing?'

'Happen you're right,' said Saddler. 'I guess we'll let them make their play first.'

Saddler counted the riders. There were eleven of them and as they gradually moved in closer to the stage, he could see that they were all of them thickly daubed with paint. At this distance, he couldn't say for sure to what tribe they belonged, but he had an idea they were Chickasaws. This boded ill. It had been a bad sign when the Chickasaws had worked with the Chiricahuas to burn down the Indian Bureau offices, and if now a war party of Chickasaws were riding openly through Choctaw territory, it meant that the whole of the territories was now hazardous. The Choctaw had been as peaceable as you like for years now, but seemingly they too had had enough and were prepared to come to terms with rival tribes, so that they could all work together with a view to driving white men from their lands.

The stage was going at a fair lick, but Saddler was holding some speed in hand for when they needed it. He hoped to give out to the men riding down on them that they were going at full pelt. It was only a tiny element of surprise, but then they needed whatever edge they could find right now. The horsemen were now less than a hundred yards from the coach, and still moving in at an angle.

Saddler heard an echoing thud, which put him greatly in mind of the noise that a woodpecker makes when it is hammering at a tree to catch a grub. He glanced round and saw the arrow which had embedded itself in the door, right in the middle of the pleasant rustic scene. He banged urgently on the roof.

'Tyler, start shooting!' he cried.

9

It was a tricky manouevre, but Saddler succeeded in tucking the reins between his knees and then raising his own rifle to his shoulder. He fired at the horses and was gratified to see one of the riders fall, as his horse turned a somersault.

'Aim at the horses,' he told Jake, who responded by saying cheerfully,

'Don't teach your grandma to suck eggs, Saddler. Me and Tyler know our work.' There was evidently something in this, because he and his brother, working in concert, brought down a couple of riders. The remaining eight men moved further away. There had been no answering fire, which gave Saddler hope that the Indians didn't have firearms. The arrow that had struck the stage was a lucky shot; it must have been at the outer limits of the range, especially from a galloping horse.

It was a stand-off, or what some would call an *impasse*. The Indians could not approach any closer to the stage without the risk of being shot, but there was no way of shaking them off. A man galloping on horseback will always be faster than four horses pulling a heavy wagon behind them. Already, Saddler could sense that his own horses were beginning to flag and were in need of slowing down. Eventually, they would have to stop to rest and then they would really be in trouble. There were only eight men on their tail now, but what if more arrived? Things were, from all that Saddler was able to collect, looking pretty desperate for them.

When he heard shots from some way away, clearly not being fired by Tyler or Jake, Saddler's spirits fell. He took it as read that this meant either that the Indians riding alongside them, or some of their allies hidden ahead, had guns.

In such a case they were done for. However, when he looked over to the riders he was astonished to see that another was down and that only seven remained in their band. Whoever had been firing had been aiming not at them but at their attackers.

The track along which they were thundering was heading down to a little valley. Scattered along the floor of this valley were heaps of boulders and scree. From the side of one of these boulders Saddler saw a puff of smoke emerge; a second later he heard the crack of a shot. As they came to the foot of the slope and began to run along the level ground of the valley floor, Saddler saw two figures ahead of him: a man and a woman. Both were waving their arms frantically, indicating that he should stop.

The shooting had discouraged the riders who had been harrying them. They were hanging back now, not so confident as they had seemed earlier. Saddler brought the stage to a halt and turned round to see what was happening. Just as though he could look into their heads and see what they were thinking, Saddler knew the calculations that were now taking place. There were seven of them, armed only with bows and knives. On this side though, were four men, all armed with rifles. It would be madness for the Indians to continue prosecuting the assault and, sure enough, they lit out, back the way they had come. Which doesn't mean to say, thought Saddler to himself, that they will not be back with their friends, some of whom might very well have guns.

Another man came out from the rocks to join the man and woman, who were standing there with looks of the greatest relief on their faces. Saddler and Jake Jackson jumped down to see who they had to thank for help in driving off the Indians. Abigail and Tyler also climbed out to see what was going on.

The man who had waved them down

looked to be about forty, as did the woman at his side. The other man was much younger, about half their age and turned out to be their son. The three of them spoke with a drawl that Saddler couldn't quite place. They certainly didn't come from any of the neighbouring states.

'I'm Leroy Clarke and this here's my wife Rose and my boy Pierre. We're mighty glad to see you folks.'

'Where you from, Mr Clarke?' asked Saddler and received the surprising answer that the family hailed from Montana.

'That's a fair walk from here,' remarked Saddler, curious. 'How'd you fetch up in this neck o' the woods?'

'Come to homestead,' said Clarke. 'Loaded up a wagon and come down here to start a farm.'

'Homestead?' asked Saddler. 'What're you talking about? This is Indian land, given 'em by treaty.'

'Yeah,' said the man, a little embarrassed from what Saddler could see. 'If you served in the army you might get a quarter section in some new territory like Nebraska, but the rest of us have to do what we can. We weren't harming anybody here, there's plenty o' room. We just built us a little soddie and then set to ploughing.'

Saddler shook his head and made an exasperated sound in his throat.

'You can't just settle on somebody's land like that. It's men like you as has got everything stirred up round here. No wonder the Indians are riled, seeing people like you steal their land.'

Leroy Clarke didn't appear to be the slightest bit put out at having his conduct denounced in this way. He spat to one side and said,

'Well, it makes no odds now. We been driven out last night. Been walking ever since, wondering how far we was goin' to get before those savages caught up with us. You boys are angels of mercy and that's a fact.'

'You want us to rescue you?' asked Saddler. 'Yeah, you people make the trouble and then look to others to pull your chestnuts out o' the fire. I don't think so.'

Even as he said this, Saddler had privately decided that the more of them in a group, the better. Five men with rifles could prove a formidable deterrent to any attacks; certainly better odds than just the three of them, as it had been earlier. He didn't intend to let the fellow think, though, that he had a right to come on board the stage. Let him plead!

'Hell's afire,' said Clarke. 'You can't mean to leave us here? What's wrong with you boys?'

The Jackson brothers had been doing some very similar figuring to Saddler's, and so he was not surprised when Tyler and Jake led him off for a private conference.

'Come on, man,' said Tyler, 'you got to see where we would do well with another pair of guns on our side.'

'Sure,' said Saddler. 'I just wanted that bastard to sweat. It's men like him who have queered the pitch for all of us who work the territories.'

When they went back to the stage it was to find that Abigail was making friends with Rose Clarke, who was surprised to find a child of such tender years travelling with a trio of rough-necks like Saddler and the Jacksons. Abigail had been a little vague about the precise circumstances, but had told the woman enough for her to be able work out that the child was no blood relative to any of the three men.

'Well, if we're goin', then we best make tracks as soon as we are able,' said Saddler. 'Abigail, come with me a minute. I have a few words to say to you.'

When they were out of earshot of the others, Abigail said anxiously, 'You're not mad at me, are you Mr Saddler?'

'Mad at you? No, nothing of the sort. I just wondered how you was bearing up, is all.'

'Oh, pretty well. That Tyler is a right funny man. He cheers me up no end.'

It was on the tip of Saddler's tongue to warn the girl not to grow too friendly with the Jacksons, but he decided against it. Tyler and Jake might be a right pair of devils in most ways, but Saddler felt that they would not harm a little girl. He even fancied that they themselves were growing fond of the child.

He contented himself with observing, 'Although I say it as shouldn't, you do know that they're a couple of rogues, don't you?'

'Oh yes,' replied Abigail. 'I think I guessed that.'

There was some little debate about the best way of arranging the new passengers. In the end, it was decided that Abigail and Mrs Clarke would naturally ride inside and that two of the men should also be inside, one either side. That would mean three men outside, which would mean that two could be on the lookout constantly for signs of danger.

Although he was markedly gruff with

Leroy Clarke, Saddler was actually quite pleased to have the extra fire-power. Of course, it would make for slower travelling with three extra bodies on board, but even without them, the stage would not realistically be able to outrun fresh galloping horses carrying only one rider. Their security lay not in speed, but strength.

Jake Jackson took it into his head to ride on the roof facing backwards, and so for the first part of the journey Saddler was stuck with Leroy Clarke sitting next to him. Having quickly established that the man knew nothing of driving a coach-and-four, and would therefore be unable to take a turn and give him a break, Saddler thought that at the least he might provide some diversion in the way of conversation.

'So what were you all doing up in Montana, meaning afore you came down here?'

'Oh, you know,' said Clarke, 'a bit of this, a bit of that.'

'No, I can't say as I do know. What do you mean?'

'I never could settle at one line of work. Always trying something new. How long you been working for Wells Fargo?'

The sudden and unexpected question took Saddler entirely by surprise.

'Wells Fargo?' he said. 'What d'you mean?'

As soon as the words were out of his mouth, he knew that he had made a false step. After all, he was driving a Wells Fargo coach. It must have looked odd to Clarke that he was taken aback by being asked about the company. He looked sidelong at the man, who had a cunning and satisfied look on his face. There was silence for a piece and then Leroy Clarke said,

'I suspicioned there was something cockeyed about this. You ain't working for Wells Fargo any more than I am. What about your friends, they in the same case?'

'For a man who has been given a free

ride,' said Saddler, 'you got a most unusual way of showin' your gratitude. What's it to you who I work for?'

'Nothing, nothing at all. Just shooting the breeze.'

There was an uncomfortable silence, which neither man was inclined to break. Saddler wondered what this fellow had been doing in Montana and why he had uprooted his family and brought them down to squat here in the Choctaw nation. There was something more than a little evasive about Leroy Clarke, and Saddler did not trust him one bit. When he sneaked another side-ways glance at the man he fancied that his face wore a gloating and satisfied expression, as though he had found an unexpected advantage some-where and was feeling pleased with himself.

The afternoon passed without any further excitement. From time to time, they passed individuals on the road; some on foot and others riding. All were Indians and none seemed to be in an aggressive frame of mind, but were simply going about their normal business. If there was a general uprising in the territories, there were still those who were not a party to it.

About halfway through the afternoon the two men in the coach swapped places with the two outside. This left Tyler sitting next to Saddler and young Pierre on the roof. Saddler chatted in a desultory fashion with Tyler Jackson, attempting from time to time to draw Pierre Clarke into the conversation, but he was a taciturn and uncommunicative youth. At one point, Tyler nudged him and when he turned, gave him an expressive look and raised his eyebrows interrogatively. Saddler interpreted this to mean, *What do you make of them folk?* He could not have formed a satisfactory answer to this question, even had it been spoken out loud. Truth was, he thought there was something not quite right about Leroy Clarke, but he was damned if he knew what it could be.

They pulled off the road for the night at the top of a rise of land. They and their coach could be seen for miles, but they in turn would be able to see anybody coming from far off. Saddler invited Abigail to help him gather wood for a fire. When they were clear of the stage and the other people, he said to the child,

'What do you make to those new passengers of ours? I would value your opinion.'

Flattered at having her views solicited in this way, Abigail thought before answering carefully,

'Mrs Clarke seems an agreeable lady. She said they had to leave where they were living in Montana because people told a lot of lies about her husband. She and her son are a little scared of him, I think.'

'What about him? What's your feeling?'

'I don't trust him. He is cunning and looks shifty.'

Saddler laughed. 'Thank you, child.

191

I'm obliged to you for that. Strikes me as you and me both have the same angle on that fellow.'

Something which Saddler noted, and later confirmed that the Jacksons had also become aware of, was that while giving practically nothing away about his own past life, Leroy Clarke appeared to be possessed of an inexhaustible desire to hear about their exploits in the Indian Territory. Cheerful and open as the Jackson brothers were normally, something about Clarke's casual enquiries set their teeth on edge and they told him nothing.

Rose Clarke filled in any awkward silences with her chatter about life in Montana, although it was still not plain just what she and her family had been doing there. At one time they had done some farming, then again, they had lived in a town for a spell. By the time everybody turned in Saddler had come to his own conclusion about Leroy Clarke, though even he could not have guessed it all.

The Jackson brothers knew this part of the country better than Saddler, so the next morning he asked their advice. According to them they were only two days' ride to Kansas by fast horse, which might equate to three or four if they stuck with the stage. This brought the conversation neatly round to what Saddler had been thinking. He and the Jacksons had walked away from the others and were just chatting in the most amiable and inconsequential fashion; leastways, that was what it would have looked like to anybody watching. In fact, the Jacksons too were growing uneasy about Clarke.

Tyler said, 'You ever meet a man who gives you the shivers, same as a snake does? That's how I feel about that fellow.'

'Me too,' said Jake. 'There's somethin' wrong about him.'

Saddler said, 'I tell you now what I think. I think he's a one who makes his livin' by finding lawbreakers and handin' them in.'

'You mean a bounty hunter?' asked Jake. 'I can't see him in that character.'

'No, you damn fool,' said Saddler, a flicker of amusement in his eyes, 'He ain't of that brand, I'll grant you. No, I mean an informer. You know the type. They report their neighbours for making a little moonshine one day. Then they hear that somebody has been stealing and tell of him too. Maybe they hang round saloons and pick up gossip. A man can scrape a living so on handouts from the sheriff and sometimes bigger reward money.'

'That's it for a bet, Saddler. You got the matter figured out right. You think he's hoping to turn us in for that stagecoach?'

'Sure he is. He knows damned well that we ain't drivin' no Wells Fargo service. More than that, he has us pegged for villains. He thinks that there'll be a reward on each of us.'

'So what's to do?' asked Jake. 'You think as we should just leave 'em out here?'

'It'd ease my mind greatly to be rid of him,' said Saddler, 'but it wouldn't sit right to dump a woman in the middle of nowhere with an Indian rising and all. Is there some way station or road house near here?'

The brothers thought about this; then Tyler said, 'There's a man runs a little drinking spot and also trades with the Indians. Mind, goin' by what we saw of the last such place, I can't say if he's still there. Anywise, it will be maybe ten miles along the road from here.'

When they started off, Saddler desired Leroy Clarke to sit alongside him as he drove. He wanted to be sure that he wasn't misjudging the man and to give Clarke the opportunity to make a more favourable impression than he had yet managed to do. Rather than that, not ten mintues after they set out, Clarke confirmed just exactly what Saddler had suspected all along. They bowled along at a fair pace, although a little more sedately than when there was only the four of them for the horses to pull.

Clarke had evidently grown weary of waiting for the others to reveal something of themselves, because he began to probe and pry. He said,

'So how come you know those other boys? You're friends or what?'

'Somethin' of the sort,' said Saddler noncommittally.

'Ah hell, you can tell me,' said Clarke. 'I'm no tattle-tale. I mind you and them's on the scout. Am I right?'

Saddler ducked his head in a bashful way, like a man whose big secret has been found out.

'Why'd you think so?' he asked.

'Stands out a mile,' Clarke cried triumphantly, pleased with himself for extracting what he saw as an admission. 'Hell, it's nothing to me. I knew when we moved down here that these parts are full of bush-whackers and bandits. You can trust me, I ain't about to tell on you all.'

'You're too sharp for me and that's a

fact,' Saddler said. 'You have a knack for knowing about such things.'

'Practice is all,' said Leroy Clark, and as soon as the words were out of his mouth, he knew that he would have done better to keep quiet. He was confirmed in this view when, without giving any notice of what he was about to do, Saddler took one hand from the reins, reached across and plucked Clarke's pistol from the holster at his hip.

'Hey,' Clarke said angrily, 'What the hell are you doing? You just give me that right back.'

Instead, Saddler cocked the piece with his thumb and pointed it straight at Leroy Clarke.

10

Saddler brought the stage to a halt, ignoring the spluttering indignation of the man seated beside him. He called to Jake, who was on the roof at the back,

'Go and relieve young Pierre of his weapon.' Jackson jumped down to comply.

Then, turning to Clarke, Saddler said, 'You get down now. Don't make any sudden movements, you hear what I say? I am not best pleased with you and it would not take much for me to get angry. You don't want that.'

Once everybody was out of the coach and the two Clarkes, father and son, had been disarmed, Saddler spoke in this way:

'I'm sorry to be disobliging, but here is where we part company with you folks.' He got no further, because Rose

Clarke cut in and began wailing and complaining.

'I thought you people were different,' said Clarke's wife. 'You are not. You're just like those we left in Montana, that is to say narrow-minded, foolish and superstitious. Every time Leroy here went off on his official duties, there was muttering and sly talk. It was enough to drive a body to drink.'

'Official duties?' asked Saddler. 'You're a regular lawman?'

Leroy Clarke was strangely reluctant to explain, but his wife displayed no such reticence.

'What my husband did was the same as if he had been a lawman. Just the next step on that road, as you might say.'

Saddler was becoming confused by all this and decided to speak straight.

'Clarke, I have you down as an informer, the sort of cur who collects reward money and suchlike. Don't you bother to deny it, now.'

Clarke did not try to deny it at all.

He said, 'So what if I picked up something on the side like that? It's just helping the law, ain't it? I knew you boys was up to no good.'

'So what's these official duties, as your wife is talkin' of?'

'Like she said, just the final step in lawing. After the sheriff catches the man and the judge deals with him, I just executed the judgement is all.'

Rose Clarke intervened at this point, saying, 'They called on my husband's services all over the state.'

'Services?' said Saddler, realization slowly dawning. 'God almighty, don't tell me you was a hangman?'

'I was,' said Clarke. 'And I ain't ashamed to own it neither. Somebody has to do the job.'

At this point Tyler Jackson could restrain himself no further.

'An informer *and* a hangman? That's surely a rare combination. I never met such a one before.'

'Nor will do again, I pray to God,' said his brother piously.

'All of which makes it more certain that we can't carry you people any further,' said Saddler. 'There is some kind of trading post a way down the road here. As for us, we are going on alone.'

'You'd abandon a woman in the middle of the wilderness?' said Rose Clarke. 'You're a fine one, I must say.'

Now the truth was, Saddler was feeling unsure about whether he was doing the right thing about this. True, Leroy Clarke was a mangy dog who deserved to be chucked out of their stage, but his wife and son were a different matter. Still, as Saddler thought about it, he had a more important consideration, which was the saving of a helpless child. He could not jeopardize that and knew that Clarke would raise an alarm and have them all arrested if he was able.

At last he said to Rose Clarke, 'You and your son may remain with us. That's as far as I can go. I have to get that there child to safety and I think that husband of yourn would hinder me in that if he could. He would sell us to Wells Fargo for the reward money.'

Clarke's wife and son would not leave him and so Saddler announced that they were off without them. He hoped that they would find shelter along the road, but his only real concern was bringing Abigail out of the territories and safe to her mother's family. Everything else would have to give way to that end, and if that meant the family of a lowdown skunk like Leroy Clarke had to be left by the wayside, then so be it.

A half-hour after leaving the Clarkes, the stage passed the little trading post that Jackson had mentioned. There were horses outside and one or two white men smoking. At the very least, the Clarkes might find some help there.

Saddler's conscience, which was as he had himself remarked to Abigail, soon after they met, not in tip-top condition, was troubling him a little about Leroy Clarke's pistol, which he had appropriated for himself. Now taking a man's horse or gun and leaving him defenceless out in the wild was generally regarded as being a pretty low trick. In most frontier parts, it was a hanging matter.

Nevertheless, since losing his own handgun to Marshal Devlin, Saddler had felt the lack keenly. He had the rifle, but that was not nearly so reassuring as the feel of a pistol right there at hand the whole time. It had been so long since he had lived without that familiar sensation that he felt undressed when he wasn't carrying, almost like he had forgotten to put his pants on or some such.

Still, Saddler's conscience had grown used over the years to being placated and having its protests ignored or overruled, and so he succeeded in stilling his qualms by reflecting that the boy Pierre had a gun. They were not wholly defenceless. The horses were being well behaved, so Saddler held the reins with just the one hand and took

Clarke's pistol from his belt. It was a strange piece of engineering; when they stopped he would have to examine it more closely. He had heard of this weapon before; some had been circulating for two years or so. It was the so-called Thuer conversion of the standard 1860 Army Colt. Instead of loading it with powder from a flask there were fiddly little brass cylinders which were fitted into the chambers. There was a plate at back of the cylinder with six little firing pins fitted to it.

One thing was for sure, he wouldn't be likely to find any more ammunition for such a strange weapon, leastways not hereabouts. He had only six shots here and he'd have to make sure that every one counted.

Jake was sitting next to Saddler, riding shotgun, and the two of them fell into conversation. Tyler was the brighter of the two Jackson brothers, but Jake was no fool.

'I knew all along as something wasn't

right about that bastard,' he said. 'Ever have that feeling when your skin crawls or the hairs at back o' your neck start tickling and you know somethin's amiss?'

'I know the feeling well enough,' replied Saddler. 'It's saved my life afore now. Listen, Jackson, we need to talk about what's to do when me and the child part company with you and Tyler.'

'Ah Saddler, why'd you be wantin' to do that? We all get along right well.'

Saddler grinned. 'I've enjoyed visiting with you boys, but all good things come to an end, or so they say. We've been on the road in this thing long enough for people to notice. Give it another day and you'll have men from Pinkertons riding down on you to get it back for Wells Fargo. No, me and the girl are going to be going on alone later today.'

'Saddler, you cowson, you know me and Tyler can't run this thing on two horses alone. You'll be leaving us in the shit and no mistake.'

'You got your horses. How much

longer you think you can ride round in a Concorde without somebody taking steps to return it to the owner?'

Jake laughed, a full bellied, boyish roar. 'I guess you're about right.'

'Tell me now, why did you and that brother of yours steal the damned thing in the first place?'

'It's like this,' said Jake, his eyes twinkling. 'Me and Tyler had a thing goin', which was seeing how big an object we could make off with. Well, horses are nothing. We stole a hundred horses. One day, Tyler steals a cow, which is a bit bigger than a horse and then after that, we took a steam engine.'

'A steam engine? What, you mean a locomotive?'

'No, of course not. That'd be crazy. No, it was something mounted on a wagon, used for pumping water out o' a mine or something. Boy, that was heavy. For a month or more, we made sure that nothing we could take would be bigger than that. Then we held up this thing and the passengers were a little rude and so we thought, what the hell? Why not steal a stagecoach?'

'One of these days you boys'll go too far.'

'Ain't happened yet,' said Jake Jackson cheerfully.

As the evening approached, Saddler brought the stage to a halt and explained his reasoning to Abigail and the Jacksons.

He said, 'If we go another ten miles in this thing without coming up against somebody who wants to take it back, then I'd be surprised. We had a good run with it, but it's time to stop now.'

'So what are you and the child going to do?' asked Tyler.

'We're going on alone,' said Saddler firmly. 'It is only a day or two now 'til we hit Kansas. The town we want is not far from the border.'

'Well, I guess that lets me and Jake out of it. We can't set foot in Kansas. They got a dozen warrants out on us.'

'Well, leastways you put some distance 'tween you and that Devlin. So have we, for the matter of that, for which I am mighty grateful.'

Jake went up to the Concorde and slapped it on the side, the way you would a horse after it's carried you a good long way.

He said, 'I'm goin' to miss this thing. It's a good way to travel.'

Saddler laughed. 'No doubt you'll steal something just as handy one day and maybe even bigger. A river-boat, perhaps?'

They unharnessed the horses and fetched out the saddles from where they were stored at the back of the coach. Abigail seemed thoughtful and a little sad to be parting from the Jackson brothers. There was no denying that Tyler and Jake could be good company, always provided you didn't have anything that they might want to steal.

After the men had taken whatever was worth salvaging from the coach they were at a loss to know what to do with the empty vehicle. Leaving it there was as good as a signpost, telling anyone who passed that they had been this way. In the end they did nothing and just let the thing stay there.

When they said farewell to each other, Abigail went up to the Jacksons and kissed both men on their cheeks.

'I hope that you keep out of trouble in the future,' she said.

The two men seemed quite affected by this, it being a good long while since any human body had expressed such a wish to them.

Before they left Tyler said to Ben Saddler, 'You take a care of that child now, Saddler. She is a special one all right.'

'I know it,' said Saddler.

Saddler and Abigail rode on for a few hours until dusk was falling and then set up camp off the road a ways.

Before they slept, Abigail said, 'Those two were nice, but I don't think they knew right from wrong.'

'You got that right. That's the one problem that those Jackson boys ever did suffer from. They are a rare breed, not wicked, but lackin' any notion of what they should or shouldn't be doing. Mind, they never harmed me none and all my dealings with 'em have been friendly enough. They're devils to cross, though.'

All that Abigail knew about her mother's family was that she had grown up in the town of Ox Creek, which was south of Wichita and right close to the border with the Indian Territories. She had never been told her mother's maiden name and all she could remember was that her mother had grown up in a big house with servants. She had formed the impression that her mother's family were very well to do.

Abigail also had some vague memory that her maternal grandfather might be a lawyer of some kind, but this was the sum total of her knowledge. That, of course, and the fact that her mother's given name was Marion.

Of course, there was no guarantee that Abigail's grandfather was still resident in Ox Creek, but that was surely the best location to begin with.

The next two days passed peaceably and the two of them saw no further signs of Indians on the war path. They were able to buy food and travel at no more than a brisk trot. It was really starting to look to Ben Saddler as though he had achieved his end and brought that poor young orphan safe out of the territories. This was a heartening and encouraging thought and he was feeling pretty braced with himself. That was until the afternoon of the second day after they parted from the Jackson brothers.

As they rode along on that sunny afternoon Saddler was entertaining Abigail with some highly edited stories of his experiences in the War between the States. She was a satisfying listener, who always gasped at the right points and knew when to smile or nod. Saddler was basking in the little girl's attention and so engrossed in his own stories that he did not notice the three men on horseback who were watching them from a grove of trees ahead. The riders were just setting dead still, which perhaps explains why he hadn't seen them, but as he later admitted, that was no sort of excuse. He should have been more alert.

The three men were Chickasaw braves and they were running from the army. Since they fully expected to be hanged, if they were caught, for what they and their friends had done to settlers on the fringes of the territories, they felt there was nothing to lose. The sight of two white travellers, ambling along through the territories like they had a perfect right to be there, was a provocation to the three warriors. They waited until the man and girl were a hundred yards from them and then set their horses in motion and galloped straight for them.

It was the movement that caught Saddler's eye, and he knew in an instant that he had been remiss and that he and the girl both might pay the forfeit for his carelessness. He pulled out the Thuer Colt, cocking it with his thumb as he did so.

To Abigail, the three figures racing towards them were like visions from a nightmare. They were so smeared and bedaubed with streaks of white paint that one could hardly see their skins. It was not only the paint; they had all somehow plastered feathers and scraps of fur over their bodies too, making them look less like men and more like some kind of monsters. On their heads they wore not feathered bonnets, but horned headdresses, maybe made from bison or something. All in all, they were the most frightening apparitions that the girl could ever have imagined.

As the lead rider was closing on them Saddler fired twice, sending the man falling backwards from his mount. None of the three were carrying firearms, only bows and light lances. Saddler's third shot took another of the Indians and he felt exultant. The last rider passed by at a distance of only ten or twelve feet and Saddler twisted to take this one as well. But the fellow was as quick as a rattlesnake. As he rushed past the man and child, he raised the bow, which had been hidden among all his feathers and pieces of fur, and let fly an arrow.

In later years, when she was a grown-up woman, it was the sound which Abigail Filer recalled most vividly about that moment. It was a hollow thud, like somebody might have struck a big iron pot with a wooden spoon or something of that sort. At first she thought that maybe the Indian had banged a drum or perhaps dropped something. Then she saw the arrow protruding from Ben Saddler's chest and knew that he had been hit and that the sound she heard was the noise of an arrow crashing into a man's body and setting his ribcage echoing. The Indian who had fired the bow at him galloped off and was soon lost to sight. Saddler just sat there quietly, without moving or saying anything, with that arrow sticking out of him.

Abigail was so frightened that she could hardly breathe. The blood was singing in her ears and she wondered if this was what it felt like when people were about to faint. Then she felt ashamed of herself, because she knew that the chief part of her fear was being left alone out in the wild without Saddler to protect her. And still the man said nothing.

Then, just when she was beginning to feel the first stirrings of hysteria, Saddler said,

'Abigail, I am hurt. I don't think I'm killed, but I'll need your help. You understand?'

'I don't know what to do. I don't know anything about nursing.'

'You don't fret about that. It's not nursing I need.'

The wounded man reached up his right hand and felt the shaft of the arrow, which was buried beneath his collarbone on the left-hand side of his chest. He felt round the flesh cautiously, wincing with pain as he did so.

His face, which had been grave, cleared a little, although he was still grimacing.

He said, 'It's not as bad as I feared. This ain't a mortal wound.'

'What can I do?'

'First off,' said Saddler, 'is where I have to get down from my horse. Then I'll tell you. Cover your ears honey, I'm goin' to squeal like a stuck hog when I move.'

Ben Saddler had not been exaggerating when he said that he would squeal. He bellowed with pain as he swung himself off the saddle and somehow got to the ground.

After he was standing by the horse he stood for a while, panting and trying to gather his resolve. His face was white and glistening with sweat. Abigail said nothing at all, feeling quite correctly that he wasn't feeling like any chatter just then.

After he seemed to have recovered a little, Saddler said, 'Listen up, Abigail. This arrow has not pierced my vitals. Nor has it struck a bone. It is wedged in the muscle, between my collarbone and my armpit. We can get it out, but it's goin' to hurt like the devil and I'll need you to do it.'

The child's breath left her body and she felt giddy. 'You want that I should dismount?' she asked.

'Yes, unless you think you can help from up there,' Saddler said with asperity. 'Abigail, what I ask is not hard. It will be a sight worse for me, but if you won't do it, I am like to die in this spot.'

With the greatest reluctance and feeling as though her limbs had turned to lead, Abigail climbed down from the pony and went over to where Saddler was standing. He was breathing heavily and his face was drawn with pain.

'All right,' he said. 'Here's the way of it. You mark that I am not bleeding much from this arrow? That's 'cause the shaft is plugging the wound. Pull it out and I'm apt to start bleeding pretty free. We need some cloth to wad up, so's we can cover the hole when the arrow comes out.'

'I can tear up my petticoat if that would be any use?'

'Good girl. Can you do that before we start?'

When Saddler talked of 'starting', Abigail felt sick again and decided to occupy herself with something practical, which would take her mind from the horror ahead. She went over to the pack on her pony and pulled out the dress and petticoat that she had been wearing when first she encountered Saddler.

Over her shoulder, she called, 'How do you want it? In strips or big pieces?'

'Do some o' both.'

The material tore easily and along straight lines. It did not take too long before she had produced a number of bandages and three large squares of cloth. While she was engaged upon this task, Abigail felt safe and could drive from her mind the thought of what soon faced her. While she fussed with tearing up the petticoat, attempting to make the pieces neater and neater, Saddler said,

'I hate to hurry you, child, but the sooner we do this, the better for us both.'

She went over to the man, who said, 'Here is what we will do. It's nothing, I done this a mort of times before. Fold up one o' them squares as small as may be.'

As the girl did so, Saddler continued. 'As soon as the arrow is out, we'll clap it on the hole.'

The matter-of-fact way that Saddler talked, referring to his wound as a 'hole', worked some effect upon the child, calming her down and making it possible for her to follow his simple instructions. When she had fashioned a wad from the torn up petticoat, Saddler said,

'Now for the next bit.' He smiled at Abigail, who was now on the verge of tears. 'Don't start crying now, I need to see what you're about.'

'What would you have me do?'

'As it stands, this arrow hasn't gone through any vein nor scratched the bone. It's gone clean into the muscle here, below my collarbone. If we can pull it straight out, then it'll leave a clean wound and it'll just be a matter o' stopping the blood flowing too freely. You follow me so far?'

'Yes. Yes I think so.'

'Now we don't want it to wiggle around as it comes out. It ain't gone through a vein or artery yet, but it could if we don't draw it out just the way it come in. That means pulling it straight out, just how it went in. Clear so far?'

'Can I ask a question?' said Abigail timidly, feeling sick, but at the same time thinking about what Saddler had been saying.

''Course you can, child. Go right ahead.'

'My father showed me some Indian arrowheads one time. I noted that they had barbs on them, to stop them falling out, once they were stuck in . . . something. Won't it tear your flesh open to pull it free?'

'Some have such barbs. Many don't. We'll have to hope this one don't. Hand me that wadding.'

Abigail watched in horrified fascination, as Saddler lay flat on his back on the ground.

He said to her, 'Come nigh to me. Now listen, if you fiddle around, I'm like to move and then the arrow head will dig in further and cause the Lord knows what mischief. I need you to grab ahold of it firmly and then pull straight up, with all your strength. Do you think you can do it?'

'I'm sure I can,' said the girl, though her heart felt as though it was pounding through her chest.

'Good. Now get yourself into a good stance. Over me there. Now, on the count of three you reach down and pull that arrow up, like you're plucking a tent peg from the ground or somethin' o' that nature. You ready?'

'I am.'

'One, two, three,' counted Saddler and no sooner had he said 'three' than the child snatched hold of the arrow and plucked it from his chest. Saddler fainted from the pain.

11

When Saddler came to, he found that he felt a lot better. The wound from the arrow was throbbing like crazy, but there was no longer a chunk of flint pressing on the nerves that ran through his shoulder. He reached up and found that Abigail had somehow managed to position the wad of cotton over the hole made by the arrow. She was sitting on the ground beside him, gazing anxiously at his face.

'Hey,' he said. 'You made a right good job o' that little bit of doctoring. I'm mighty obliged to you.'

'Do you feel any better?'

'Yes, heaps better. We had best stay here for the night though. I don't mind that I'll be much use in the saddle for a few hours yet.'

'Would you like me to fetch your blanket and lay it over you?'

'That'd be nice. Thanks.'

And so it was that the two of them spent the night right there by the road, in plain view of anybody who passed by. Fortunately, nobody *did* travel along the road that night and they were left unmolested.

When he woke in the morning the first thing that Saddler did was to flex his fingers and clench his fist. His chief fear now was that some infection would have set in and that he would be going down with blood poisoning. There was no sign of this, at least not yet, and the only sensations were the quite natural ones of stiffness and pain from having had his muscle sliced open by a razor-sharp piece of stone.

Saddler examined the arrow, which Abigail had dropped as soon as she had extracted it from his shoulder. The head was chipped from flint, which was unusual these days. Combined with the way that those boys had been tricked out in feathers and mud, it struck

Saddler that they must have eschewed modern customs and determined to rely only upon their traditional ways in battle. This would also account for why none of the warriors he had encountered in the last week or so had been carrying or using firearms. He suspected that this was tied up with some sort of ghost-dance nonsense and that those taking part in the uprising had been led to believe that their ancestors would help them, if only they rejected the ways of the white man.

By Saddler's reckoning, if they rode hard this day they would be in reach of Ox Creek by nightfall. There'd be no point in wandering round a strange town at night asking a heap of questions, so they would probably need to spend one more night out in the open. With luck though, that would be the last of it and he would be able to deliver the child to her family tomorrow and his mission would be accomplished.

What then? Well, he had the money

from the sale of the whiskey, more or less intact. He felt sure that he could pick up something in Ox Creek that would be like to fetch a good price back in the territories. One thing was for sure: he'd be giving a wide berth to the Chickasaw and Choctaw nations both. He would stick to the Seminole and Creek for a spell.

Abigail woke a little later and then, recollecting the events of the previous day, she looked anxiously at him.

'Do you feel better today, Mr Saddler?' she asked.

'Much, thank you. What about you? Were you all right after doin' that little bit o' surgery on me?'

'Well, I was . . . sick.' She blushed. 'Awful sick. Mind, I did it right, didn't I?'

'That you did, Abigail, that you did. I don't think there's many girls your age as could have done what you did. I cannot tell you what I owe you.'

'Well though, you have done a lot for me, looking after me and such. It's only right that I should help you when I am able.'

They didn't speak for a minute or two and then Saddler said thoughtfully, 'Thinking it over and takin' everything into account, I would say that the balance sheet is pretty even on both sides. It's true as I rescued you from that wood and so on, but then again you freed me from imprisonment and saved my life last night. No, I would say that we are square and neither owes anything.'

He smiled. 'And let me tell you now, child, I never thought to say such a thing to a twelve year-old girl. But fair's fair. You done as good as any grown-up person could. I don't say that lightly, neither.'

The child glowed with pleasure at this unlooked-for praise. Then she said,

'You think we should kind of bandage up your shoulder for the ride?'

'Yeah, I think that's just what we ought to do. I might need to call on your services again there, on account of

I can't reach round behind me too well just now.'

Eventually they managed to wind a strip of cloth round Saddler's shoulder and use it to hold in place another pad of cloth. The wound began leaking again while they did this and Saddler was hoping that the bleeding wouldn't keep going too long. Even a small wound can cause a man to faint from blood loss if the bleeding goes on for long enough. He had seen this many times during the war.

That day passed uneventfully as they proceeded partly at a walk, interspersed with trotting. He didn't like to say anything that might alarm the child, but Saddler was worrying that the wound was not closing up and that unless he was able to spend some time completely immobile, then the blood would continue to flow. He couldn't see a remedy for this. They were almost out of provisions and what they had left would last until the evening. He hoped that his calculations were accurate and that they would reach Ox Creek the next day. Whatever else befell them them there, they might at least be able to buy some food.

Abigail sensed that something was amiss, because after their midday stop she asked him outright, 'Is your shoulder troubling you?'

'To speak plainly, it is. Now listen. The pain I can bear. I've had worse. Problem is, losing all this blood. I hope it'll stop, but if it don't, then I might pass out.'

'Oh Mr Saddler,' said Abigail, 'I won't leave you if that happens. You may depend upon it.'

'Why, you young fool,' Saddler said roughly, 'that's the very thing you got to do, if that happens.' He could see the hurt in her eyes at being spoken to so harshly and Saddler tried to smooth it over.

'Abigail, I have to speak straight now. If I sound rough, then I'm sorry. You have to get yourself to Ox Creek. I hope to take you there, but if'n I can't, then you'll have to get there by your own self. You understand?'

'I guess,' said the child uncertainly. 'Although I don't know the way.'

'That's nothing. You just carry on down this road and after a good long pace, you'll come to a crossway. You take the right turn, which'll lead you along the road you want. We're almost clear of the territories now; in fact we might already be in Kansas.'

Still, the girl looked as though she hadn't quite grasped his meaning and so Saddler put matters even more bluntly.

'If this blood loss gets worse, I could die. You'd be left alone at the mercy of Lord knows who. There's no point thinking of me, you must take a care of your own self. You know it's true, Abigail.'

The girl said nothing and then, in a very quiet voice, she conceded, 'I guess. But let's hope it does not come to that.'

During the rest of the day Saddler

fancied that things were a little better. The bleeding appeared to have slowed right down and the wound was clotting. He was greatly relieved at this, not so much for his own sake as that it meant that Abigail would not be left defenceless and alone. By the time that it was getting dark, they had reached the crossroads that he had described to Abigail. The road ahead led to Wichita and the right fork, if his memory served him right, should take them to Ox Creek.

They moved a little way from the road that last night and settled down in a little stand of pines, just far enough from the crossroads for passing travellers to be unlikely to spot them.

The next day they were plumb out of provisions.

''Less I'm greatly mistook, we are only five miles from Ox Creek,' Saddler said. 'I'm sorry there's nothing to eat, Abigail, but we've plenty of cash money and as soon as we hit town I'll get us something. The best dodge now is to push on and see how soon we can get to Ox Creek.'

It was during that last stretch of the journey, when you might have thought that it was all finished that Saddler came near to losing his life. It was the most stupid thing imaginable. Abigail's pony had been showing signs of tiredness. Perhaps he wasn't used to such long rides, but that morning he was particularly skittish. An hour after they started out, the beast bucked and damned near threw his rider. Saddler moved in fast and grabbed the reins, whereupon the pony bolted. Saddler managed to keep hold of the reins and stop the creature charging down the road, but in so doing he was twisted awkwardly and felt a weird stabbing pain on his left side. He knew at once that the wound had opened up again.

There was no purpose in telling the child of this and so they just carried on down the road. Saddler was uncomfortably aware that his shirt was growing sticky and wet. There was no more material left, so there was nothing for it but to forge on.

* * *

The town of Ox Creek lay on the banks of the Arkansas river. It was a bustling little place, with neatly painted white clapboard houses and a main street with brick-built stores and churches. Saddler was feeling distinctly unwell by the time they hit the centre of town and did not really want to get down from his horse in case, once down, he could not find the strength to mount it again. He reined in outside a bakery and gave Abigail enough to buy a loaf of bread. For his own part, he was not at all hungry.

While the child was in the shop Saddler accosted one or two passers-by and asked if any of them recalled a girl named Marion, who had grown up in the town and whose father might be a lawyer, living in a large house. The two men and a woman whom he accosted

233

in this way gave him very strange looks and shook their heads. Saddler knew that he presented a dreadful sight, with blood now staining half his shirt. No wonder those folk didn't feel like chatting to him; he must look a regular scarecrow!

When Abigail came out of the baker's Saddler was all but spent. He made one last effort by calling to an old fellow who looked somewhat like some Biblical prophet, with a long white beard and sharp blue eyes.

'Excuse me, sir,' said Saddler. 'I'm looking for the house of a man who had a daughter called Marion. She left here to get married, maybe fourteen years back? He might live in a big house?'

'Marion Gilchrist,' said the man promptly, 'She ain't living there now though. Like to break her father's heart, went off with a missioner.'

'That's the fellow,' Saddler said eagerly. 'Where does he live?'

'Why, down yonder,' said the old man, pointing with a walking cane. 'You can see his house from here. See that little turret, with a lightning rod atop of it? That's the Gilchrist place.'

Abigail had turned pale at hearing this. When she remounted the pony and was eating dry bread, Saddler said to her, 'Ain't you pleased, child? We're nearly done.'

'I don't know my grandfather,' she said in a small voice. 'I know you. I don't know that I want to go and live there.'

'That's a lot of foolishness. Come on.'

Saddler led the way to the big house, but the nearer they got to it the more it seemed to recede in his vision. This is damned odd, he thought to himself, we don't look to be getting any closer. At last they reached the place and Saddler, making one last effort, managed to slither down from his saddle. It was all he could do to stand upright and he observed that his pants too were now damp with blood.

Abigail too dismounted and the two

of them stood looking at the imposing mansion. He felt the child's hand slip into his own and he gave it a reassuring squeeze.

'Don't worry, it'll be fine,' he said. 'I'll be bound that your grandpa's a fine gentleman.'

12

In books, reunions of this sort between long-lost relatives are usually of an affecting character and generally entail the various parties falling into each other's arms with a good deal of weeping and kissing. This was by no means the case here, at least not to begin with. Not being versed in social niceties, Saddler made a grave error to begin with by taking what he saw as the obvious course of action, which is to say: walking up to the front door and knocking on it.

He soon discovered from the starchy and dignified woman who answered the door that this was not at all the correct proceeding. She took one look at the ragged and unkempt pair in front of her and curtly directed them to go at once round to the tradesman's entrance. She thought Abigail was a boy and not unnaturally assumed them both to be beggars of some description.

When once they reached the kitchen door Saddler compounded his felony by entering the house unbidden and seating himself at once at the scrubbed deal table. He knew that if he did not do so then he was liable to collapse on the spot. This caused some intakes of breath and an audible gasp from the cook, who had never heard of such a liberty before from any of the hobos and bums who received handouts from the household.

Saddler was in no mood to delay though, fearing that he would pass out before he had been able to set the business out.

'This here is Marion Gilchrist's daughter,' he announced, without any preamble. 'She is the grand-daughter of him as owns this house. Her ma and pa are dead and this here is the only family as she has.'

This sensational statement had

hardly had time to register before Saddler followed it up with an even more amazing performance, which consisted in his losing consciousness, slumping sideways and then falling, apparently lifeless, to the floor of the kitchen.

When he came to, Saddler could not at first make out where he was and what the strange bodily sensations which he was experiencing might mean. It took him some time to realize that it was no more than the pleasant feeling of crisp, clean sheets around him and a soft mattress beneath. He opened his eyes and saw the most beautiful woman he had ever seen in his life. She was wearing a dove grey dress and sat at the side of the bed, gazing at him thoughtfully.

He was sensible of the impropriety of lying in bed like this in the presence of a lady and made as if to rise, but she put out a warning hand.

'Don't move, Mr Saddler. You have lost a great deal of blood. We don't want that wound opening up again.'

'I'm sorry ma'am, you have the advantage of me. I'm not sure where I am, nor who you are?'

'I'm Abigail's aunt.'

For Saddler, the word 'aunt' had always conjured up elderly spinsters or middle-aged matrons. The thought that this vision of loveliness could be anybody's aunt was a peculiar one.

The woman continued, 'As to where you are, you are in my house, or I should say my father's house.' He still looked puzzled and so she continued,

'Abigail's mother was my big sister. She was ten years older than me. There was an estrangement between my father and her after her marriage and so we have not heard from her these thirteen years or so. We were not aware that she had had a child.'

'Well, ma'am, I'm right grateful for your help. I hope I'll not impose too long on your hospitality. I feel better already.'

'Impose on our hospitality? How can

you be so absurd? We have heard from Abigail something of her adventures. Do you honestly imagine for a moment that we would turn you out of our home after all that?'

She seemed offended that Saddler could even hint at such a thing. 'Anyway, I promised that I would tell my niece as soon as you were awake. I'll go and fetch her.'

'How long have I been here ill?'

'You were unconscious for two days. Our doctor despaired of your life at one point. Let me call Abigail.'

When Abigail entered the room she was no longer wearing the shirt and pants in which she had made the greater part of her journey across the Indian Territories. He saw a demure little girl wearing a modest black dress and with her hair properly tended to. It was hard to think of such a person torching Fort Renown!

When she entered the room Abigail ran at once to the bed and threw her arms round Saddler.

'Oh Mr Saddler, I'm so glad to see you awake. They told me that you might die, but I didn't believe a word of it. I knew things would turn out all right; they always do, you know.'

'So you are finding yourself in a good situation here?' asked Saddler. 'You will be happy to stay here?'

'My aunt is the most lovely person you ever met. Grandfather is different, but I think he is kind really. He just does not like it to be known.'

'Well, child, I can't tell you how glad I am to see you settled. I can leave here with a clear conscience and it's not often I can say that.'

'Leave here? Didn't Carrie, my aunt you know, tell you? Nobody wants you to leave. They say you can stay. I'll have to go to school and learn all sorts of disagreeable things, such as how to be a lady and such like, but you must not think of going anywhere.'

'I'm not sure how your grandpa would take to that, Abigail.'

'But it was his idea. You don't want

to go wandering off again, do you? Please don't.'

'I'd best see what your grandpa has to say. As to wandering off and roamin' and such, no I can't say as I do just now. I wouldn't mind at all staying in one spot, leastways for now.'

The interview with the old man was not as alarming as Saddler had expected. Mr Gilchrist was not only a lawyer, he was a judge and he was under no illusions at all as to what kind of man Saddler was. He was, though, a man who believed in paying his debts and he knew that Saddler had put him under an obligation that could never be fully satisfied. He was a plain speaker and laid things out for Saddler.

'You wouldn't, I imagine, wish to live in a house such as this, Mr Saddler. That might not meet either of our requirements. I doubt you would wish to be sitting down to dinner with a judge every evening. I have some other properties in the town, small houses. One is vacant and you are welcome to move into it as soon as you are on your feet again.'

'I have some money sir . . . ' began Saddler, but here Judge Gilchrist broke in with the greatest irascibility.

'Devil take you, man, I don't wish to hear of money. You have done me the greatest service any man ever did in the whole course of my life and you offer me money? We will talk later of what we can do to fix you up with some employment. I have no idea what your talents incline you towards; you'll find little scope in Ox Creek for the sort of shenanigans you were up to in the territories.'

Before he left, Judge Gilchrist took Saddler's hand and said, 'From the bottom of my heart, Mr Saddler, I thank you for what you have done for me. I can never sufficiently repay you, but I'll have a damned good try.'

That evening, before he went to sleep, there was a knock at his door. Saddler called out, 'Come in,' and Abigail entered the room. He was pleased to see her again, after feeling he had to be so formal and polite with Gilchrist and his daughter. He was relaxed in Abigail's company, regarding her almost as an old comrade. Saddler was sorry to see that the child looked a little sad and he asked what was wrong.

'It's like this, Mr Saddler,' she said. 'My grandfather said that he thought you might be the type to up and run after a space and that I should perhaps not grow too fond of you, for I would then be grieved when it happened. I suppose I thought that you wanted to stay in this town for good. Was I wrong?'

Saddler called the child to him and desired her to sit on the bed.

'Abigail,' he said, 'I have spent most all my life travellin' round and never setting in one place for long. I tell you now, I am weary of it. Nothing would delight me more than settling here and working at a real job. I will not be digging up and leaving unexpectedly. I will stay for as long as you wish.'

Abigail flung her arms around Saddler and for a moment, they held each other tight. Then she bade him goodnight and left the room.

We do hope that you have enjoyed reading this large print book.

Did you know that all of our titles are available for purchase?

We publish a wide range of high quality large print books including:
Romances, Mysteries, Classics
General Fiction
Non Fiction and Westerns

Special interest titles available in large print are:
The Little Oxford Dictionary
Music Book, Song Book
Hymn Book, Service Book

Also available from us courtesy of Oxford University Press:
Young Readers' Dictionary
(large print edition)
Young Readers' Thesaurus
(large print edition)

For further information or a free brochure, please contact us at:
Ulverscroft Large Print Books Ltd.,
The Green, Bradgate Road, Anstey,
Leicester, LE7 7FU, England.
Tel: (00 44) **0116 236 4325**
Fax: (00 44) **0116 234 0205**

SHOOTOUT IN CANYON DIABLO

Steve Hayes

Canyon Diablo offers Lute Latimore a fresh start . . . provided he can live long enough to enjoy it! The plan is simple — go to work as a deputy for his brother Heck, the town marshal. But Canyon Diablo is a hell town, with a reputation for chewing up lawmen, and Lute becomes a target as soon as he pins on the star. One night, a fusillade of bullets changes everything, and suddenly a new trail beckons Lute — a killing trail . . .

GARRETT'S TRAIL TO JUSTICE

Terrell L. Bowers

Dayton Garrett is a roving trouble-shooter, taking on jobs from town-taming to bringing down a counterfeiting ring. Charged with searching for a missing child, he fetches up in Shilo, where his attorney brother Knute provides him with helpful information — and requests a favour in return. Alyson Walsh has been convicted of murder in a kangaroo court, and faces the noose in two days' time. Knute wants her broken out of jail while he endeavours to get her a fair trial — and Dayton is just the man for the job . . .

QUINCY'S QUEST

Jay Clanton

Down on his luck, Martin Quincy falls in with crooked company, and agrees to participate in a train robbery. The hold-up is successful, netting Quincy over three thousand dollars. But later he's shocked to discover that one of the other thieves shot a woman in front of her child — and when he castigates them, they beat him, steal his money, and leave him for dead in the desert. Quincy, however, is made of stern stuff — and swears to track them down and kill every one of them . . .